D0865984

Books should be returned or renewed by the last
date above. Renew by phone **03000 41 31 31** or
online *www.kent.gov.uk/libs*

J. F

C334683313

EVER DARK

ABI ELPHINSTONE

SIMON & SCHUSTER

First published as a paperback in Great Britain in 2019
by Simon & Schuster UK Ltd
This edition published in Great Britain in 2021

Text Copyright © Abi Elphinstone 2019
Interior and cover illustrations Copyright © Carrie May 2019
The Unmapped Chronicles logo Copyright © Patrick Knowles 2019

The right of Abi Elphinstone, Carrie May and Patrick Knowles
to be identified as the author and illustrators of this work respectively
has been asserted by them in accordance with sections 77 and 78
of the Copyright, Designs and Patents Act, 1988.

1 3 5 7 9 10 8 6 4 2

Simon & Schuster UK Ltd
1st Floor, 222 Gray's Inn Road
London
WC1X 8HB

www.simonandschuster.co.uk

Simon & Schuster Australia, Sydney
Simon & Schuster India, New Delhi

A CIP catalogue record for this book is available from the British Library.

ISBN: 978-1-4711-9470-2

This book is a work of fiction. Names, characters, places and incidents
are either the product of the author's imagination or are used
fictitiously. Any resemblance to actual people living or
dead, events or locales is entirely coincidental.

Typeset by M Rules
Printed and bound by CPI Group (UK) Ltd, Croydon, CR0 4YY

MIX
Paper from
responsible sources
FSC® C020471

For Gilbert,
who is every bit as brilliant as Smudge.

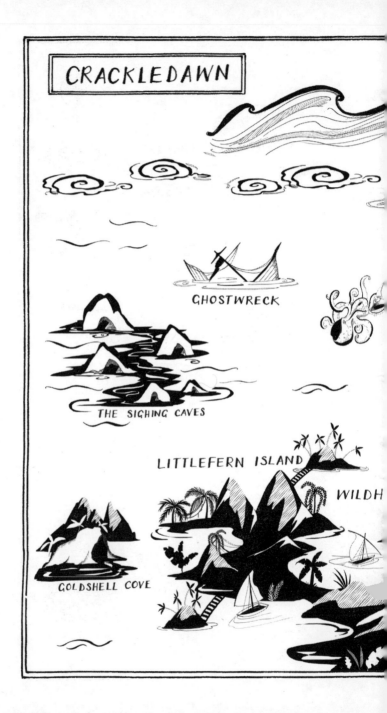

The maps you know hold well-known lines,
Shapes scored and inked in olden times.
Continents drawn and oceans named,
Peaks climbed and countries claimed.
But maps hold secrets yet untold
Of places we should ink in gold,
Up north, down south, far west and east
Kingdoms full of magical beasts.
Lands like these are hard to find
Unless you've got a curious mind ...

Prologue

The trouble with grown-ups is that they always think they're right – about bedtimes and vegetables mostly, but also about beginnings. And, in particular, about the beginnings of our world. They have all sorts of ideas about big bangs and black holes, but if they had come across the Unmapped Kingdoms (which they wouldn't have because secret kingdoms are notoriously hard to find), they would have learned that at the very, very beginning there was just an egg. A rather large one. And out of this egg, a phoenix was born.

On finding itself all alone, it wept seven tears, which, as they fell, became our continents. These lands, known as the Faraway, were dark and empty places, so, many years later, the phoenix scattered four of its golden feathers across the world and out of these grew secret – unmapped – kingdoms, invisible to those who would go on to live in the Faraway, but holding all the magic needed to conjure sunlight, rain and snow, and every untold wonder behind the weather, from the music of a sunrise to the stories of a snowstorm.

Now the phoenix, being the wisest of all magical creatures, knew that if used selfishly, magic grows strange and dark, but if it is used for the greater good it can nourish an entire world and keep it turning. So the phoenix decreed that those in the Unmapped Kingdoms could enjoy all the wonders that its magic brought, but only if they, in turn, worked to send some of this magic out into the Faraway so that the continents there might be filled with light and life. If the Unmappers ever stopped sharing their magic, the phoenix warned, both the Faraway and the Unmapped Kingdoms would crumble to nothing.

The phoenix placed the Lofty Husks in charge of each Unmapped Kingdom – wizards born under the same eclipse and marked out from the other Unmappers on account of their wisdom, unusually long life expectancy and terrible jokes – and, although in each kingdom the Lofty Husks took a different form, they ruled fairly, ensuring that every day the magic of the phoenix was passed on to the Faraway.

The Unmappers in Rumblestar collected marvels – sunlight, rain and snow in their purest form – which dragons carried on to the other three kingdoms so the inhabitants there could mix these marvels with magical ink to create weather scrolls to send on to the Faraway: sun symphonies in Crackledawn, rain paintings in Jungledrop and snow stories in Silvercrag. Little by little, the Faraway lands came alive: plants, flowers and trees sprang up and so strong was the magic that eventually animals appeared and, finally, people.

Years passed and the phoenix looked on from Everdark, a place so remote and out of reach that not even the Unmappers knew where it lay. But a phoenix cannot live forever. And so, after five hundred years, the first phoenix died and, as is the way with such birds, a new phoenix rose from its ashes to renew the magic in the Unmapped Kingdoms and continue to watch over its creations.

Time went by and the Unmappers grew to understand that every five hundred years a new era began and, as long as the phoenix showed itself to them on the night of its rising, the magic would be renewed and all would be well. Everyone believed things would continue this way forever ...

When you're dealing with magic, though, **forever** is rarely straightforward. There is always someone, somewhere, who becomes greedy. And when a heart is set on stealing magic for personal gain suddenly ancient decrees and warnings slip quite out of mind.

But that, I suppose, makes room for stories and for unexpected heroes and unlikely heroines. Because even those born in magical kingdoms can feel unimportant and overlooked, and sometimes it takes a story to show that the truly extraordinary people in this world – the ones who defeat monsters and save kingdoms – are, very often, the ones that nobody notices at first.

So grab your compass and roll down your sail – the first adventure in the Unmapped Chronicles is about to begin …

Chapter 1

It was midnight in Crackledawn – a
midnight full of magic. Sea dragons stirred
in the depths of the ocean, rock goblins
gathered in Wildhorn bay and a silver
whale surfaced beneath a moon so big
and round it was a miracle that it still hung
in the sky. And, for people like you and
me, that might well have been enough
magic to make our eyes pop and our legs
wobble. But in the Unmapped Kingdoms
there is a deeper magic still, a magic
so old and full of wonder that even the
sea dragons themselves honour it. And it

was **this** magic that the elves on board
the dhow moored up in the bay, and the
people curled up in their hammocks on the
surrounding islands, were waiting for.

'Any moment now,' the elf at the bow of
the ship whispered.

She was smaller than the rest of
Crackledawn's Lofty Husks and very round,
but her ears were so long and pointed,
even for elf ears, that you could have hung
a coat on them. She hopped from one foot
to the other and the elves sitting round the
chessboards on deck hurried towards her.
A cluster of velvet cloaks, wild white hair
and wrinkles, the Lofty Husks watched the
sky for the sign that all was well with the
Unmapped Kingdoms and the Faraway.

'Do you think this Rising will be as
brilliant as the last one?' another elf asked
as he twizzled his wiry eyebrows. 'I saw
the whole silhouette of the phoenix as
it crossed the moon before flying on to

8

the other kingdoms! Five hundred years ago, but I still remember it like it was yesterday ...'

'The Rising before that was the best, I thought,' the round elf said. 'The phoenix scattered so much stardust from its wings that you couldn't look at the night sky without blinking! What do you think **this** Rising will bring, Greyhobble?'

An elf with a monocle, a walking stick and a beard so long he had tucked it into his cloak pocket smiled. 'What will be will be.' He paused. 'But I must confess I do have high hopes for something rather splendid tonight. This is the Rising, after all, a promise from the phoenix that its magic still runs through our kingdoms. And the fact that we are always lucky enough to have the first sighting in Crackledawn, means you can count on it being nothing short of spectacular.'

Greyhobble stroked his beard. 'I mean,

without the Rising, the Unmapped Kingdoms would fall and then who would write the weather scrolls for the Faraway? All those continents left to perish – North America, South America, Europe, Africa, Antarctica, Asia and ...' He hesitated. 'What's the one with all the kangaroos again?'

'Australasia,' the elf with the woolly eyebrows prompted.

'Thank you, Timberdust.' Greyhobble straightened up. 'The phoenix entrusted Crackledawn to send sunlight to the Faraway – the very thing that first gave life to the plants, flowers and trees there – so do I think there will be silhouettes and stardust in store for us tonight? Of course! And maybe more. Who knows? We might even catch a glimpse of the phoenix's golden feathers before it flies on to Jungledrop.'

The Lofty Husks fell silent and watched the moonlight glitter on the sea because they knew better than anyone that a moment of hush was needed to let deep magic in. The silence swelled, the night breathed in and then a breeze drifted through Crackledawn.

It reached the smaller islands first, rustling through the leaves of the palm trees and slipping over the skin of the people who sat, wide-eyed and tingling with awe, in the hammocks strung between branches. Every single one of these people had been born from the sea – washed ashore on the island of Wildhorn as infants in conches – and though they could outswim the strongest currents, sail as fast as the wind and even sprout gills for a few minutes if they chose to swallow a watergum, they slept in hammocks on land because Wildhorn and its surrounding islands had come to feel like home.

The people sat in silence, bundled up in

their quilts. The Lofty Husks might have seen many Risings before but for the Unmappers in the hammocks, this was a once-in-a-lifetime event and even the breeze seemed to whisper in wonder. It skimmed across the wooden walkways that led from the smaller pieces of land to Wildhorn, the central island of Crackledawn and the one with the horseshoe bay that sheltered the fleet of dhows used by Sunraiders.

Wildhorn was also home to a number of unusual caves: a ramshackle grotto-turned-pub called the Cheeky Urchin, which the rock goblins ran; an enormous cavern, full of bubbling cauldrons and desks crowded with parchment, known as the Den, where all the sun-chatter – the tiny gold jewels found glittering on the sea floor that whispered the magical sounds of the sun – was stored; and the Warren, dozens of smaller caves connected by winding passageways, containing tables,

chairs, leather-bound books and spinning
globes, where the Lofty Husks taught
young Unmappers how to become a
Sunraider (those who captained boats
and roamed the seas for sun-chatter), or
a Sunsmith (those who mixed sun-chatter
with marvels to make ink for the Faraway's
sun scrolls).

The breeze scurried across the deck
of the elves' ship, knocking over several
chess pieces, before trailing out to sea. But
something lingered in its wake. Something
dark and unfamiliar.

One by one the Lofty Husks sniffed
the air.

'Smells like a strange sort of magic,'
Greyhobble whispered. 'You don't think—'

His words were cut short by gasps and
cheers from those in the hammocks as
the moonlight darkened. To the rest of the
Unmappers, the night was unfolding just as
they'd imagined and so the elves watched

on with narrow eyes, hoping that the strange wind meant nothing.

But the silhouette of a phoenix did not appear against the moon. Instead, a darkness crept over it, blotting out its light completely. The night deepened and then there was a screech – a bone-shaking, spine-shivering shriek – that tore through the sky like a knife.

One or two children cried out and the rock goblins gathered on the shore of Wildhorn scrambled into their burrows and disappeared from sight. Then the darkness pulled back from the moon and for several seconds the air pulsed with the thrum of beating wings. Soon this sound faded, too, and once again there was silence.

Greyhobble clutched the side of the ship. Something was wrong. Very wrong.

'It ... it **could** have been the phoenix rising,' the round elf stammered. 'If you were squinting and covering your eyes and not really looking at the moon at all ...'

'No, Crumpet,' Timberdust said in a trembling whisper. 'You know as well as I do that whatever we just witnessed smelled of dark magic.' He tightened his cape around him. '**Something** rose from the forests of Everdark tonight, but it was most certainly not a phoenix – and, if it wasn't a phoenix, what does that mean for the Unmapped Kingdoms? And the Faraway? Phoenix magic is what holds everything together!'

'Hush now, Timberdust.' Greyhobble adjusted his monocle. 'We are the Lofty Husks responsible for this kingdom so we must not panic. The fact that we are still standing, and Crackledawn is, too, means all is not lost. Yet. It's usually a few hours before sightings of the Rising are reported in Jungledrop, so we'll use our enchanted mirror rings to communicate with the Lofty

Husks in the other kingdoms and share what we have seen, then we'll captain a fleet of boats to scour the seas for any signs of dark magic. And tomorrow, we'll send the sun scrolls on to the Faraway as usual, because we made an oath to share our magic and we are not going to break it now.'

At his words the rest of the elves stood a little taller, remembering their role and the importance of the work of the Unmapped Kingdoms.

'We'll need to ban Sunraiders roaming the seas until we can be sure it's safe,' Greyhobble continued, 'but we've got enough sun-chatter stored for the Sunsmiths to use and the Sunraiders can work with us on protective enchantments. But, for the sake of the rest of the Unmappers **and** the magical beasts in this kingdom, we Lofty Husks must do what we do best.'

Crumpet frowned. 'Chess? Or ballroom dancing?'

Greyhobble rolled his eyes. 'It's hardly the time for a foxtrot below deck, Crumpet. No, now is the time –' he paused – 'to be bossy.'

The tips of Greyhobble's ears wiggled, then he tapped his mouth twice with his index finger – casting an easy spell that granted him a booming voice. He took a deep breath.

'Sunraiders and Sunsmiths! Rock goblins and sand sprites! Water pixies and cockle imps!'

Greyhobble's voice echoed across the water and the people in the palm trees, who had been whispering nervously to one another, fell silent.

'Do not be alarmed by what you have seen. The Rising might not have unfolded as expected, but rest assured we Lofty Husks will work tirelessly to find out what has happened, so that no one comes to any harm.' He paused.

'Nonetheless, until a proper plan is set in place, we ask that all Sunraiders refrain from roaming the seas and report to Timberdust, with your spell books, outside the Cheeky Urchin at sunrise tomorrow. For Sunsmiths, it will be business as usual. And please can all under-agers meet Crumpet in the Warren to practise charms and hexes against dark magic. But in the meantime –' Greyhobble thought of the bossiest thing he could possibly say – 'please go straight to sleep.'

Now, there are two types of children, both here in the Unmapped Kingdoms and back home in the Faraway, where you are now. There are those who, when told to go to sleep, close their eyes and nod off soon after. Then there are others who, upon hearing those words, close their eyes, then find themselves dangling from a drainpipe a few minutes later. And the girl with the silver nose ring, dark eyes and scruffy black

hair who, as others around her did their
best to fall asleep, began to clamber out
of her hammock was, most certainly, a
drainpipe-dangler.

Smudge shuffled to the end of her
hammock, then manoeuvred herself on
to the rope ladder dangling from it. She
placed a foot on the first rung, then began
climbing down quietly and carefully –
which was pointless really because the
monkey curled up on the pillow in her
hammock was not asleep, as she thought,
but watching her with about as much
enthusiasm as a fly who knows it's going to
get squashed.

Unaware of the monkey's gaze,
Smudge carried on climbing down, her
mind whirling with what she'd seen that
night. While everyone else sitting in their
hammocks among the palm trees had
gasped and burrowed under their quilts
on hearing the terrible screech earlier,

Smudge had kept watching the sky – and she had seen something that it seemed all the others had missed: a large black-winged creature heading out across the sea towards Lonecrag, the rock many miles north of Wildhorn where the most mysterious of sea monsters were rumoured to dwell.

The winged creature hadn't been a phoenix, Smudge was sure of that, because its shape bore no resemblance to the drawings of the phoenix that Crumpet – the Lofty Husk in charge of educating first-formers – had shown in Beast Anatomy class. This was something else and Smudge wanted to investigate further.

You see, Smudge's mind had a sideways quality to it, never quite managing to focus on the things it was meant to be focusing on. She understood that sunlight was full of secret noises, mostly missed by those in the Faraway, and that it took Sunsmiths years to work out how many hiccups, sneezes, giggles and hums made up the perfect sunrise or sunset. But, while the rest of her class took notes on this, Smudge was most likely to be found watching a glow-in-the-dark lizard scampering through the cave or a silk bat shuffling in the shadows. She was intensely interested in the world around her, but that didn't seem very helpful when trying to keep up in class.

Her spelling was terrible, her handwriting looked like a series of squashed spiders and, when it came to end-of-year exams or any sort of work that meant organising her thoughts and writing them down, she always ended up bottom of the class. Crumpet had tried to bolster Smudge's spirits, but even she couldn't stop Smudge's classmates sniggering when Smudge accidentally wrote her letters upside down on the chalkboard. Nobody seemed to want to be her friend and not even the monkey that the Lofty Husks had given her last year as a 'positive influence' could stop her being late for class, daydreaming through lessons and forgetting her belongings wherever she went.

Smudge's greatest dream was to head out in a dhow like the Sunraiders with one eye on the ship's lantern, which glowed gold whenever the vessel sailed over sunchatter, and the other on the glorious open sea. But the first time she stepped on board a dhow with her class she'd immediately forgotten everything she'd learned, leading to a steering 'incident' where she had crashed into a reef. Then, on the day she actually remembered how to steer, a minor lapse in concentration had caused her to forget to swallow a watergum before diving for sun-chatter and she had very nearly drowned.

Every child in Crackledawn was supposed to choose between being a Sunraider or a Sunsmith when they turned sixteen, but Smudge couldn't help wondering whether she was born to do something completely different. Something that might involve her sketches of the diamond-shelled turtles she had discovered on Littlefern Island, or the imagined maps she had drawn of the unexplored lands beyond the Northswirl, the legendary stretch of ocean and the boundary of Crackledawn that nobody had managed to sail beyond and return.

But, when Smudge had tried to raise the idea of an alternative path for her future, Crumpet had dismissed the notion and her classmates had dissolved into giggles. And so, little by little, Smudge's hopes and dreams of one day achieving something – **anything** – dried up and she came to accept that being lonely and a little bit useless was just part of her everyday life.

And then the Rising didn't happen.

Smudge knew she'd noticed something important. Greyhobble hadn't mentioned anything during his speech, so did that mean he'd missed it? The elf had promised that no harm would come to anyone, but if he **hadn't** seen the winged creature heading towards Lonecrag, or felt sure of the darkness in its soul as Smudge had, how could he know that everything would be okay? Perhaps Smudge could be the one to help the Lofty Husks come up with a plan to rid the kingdom of this creature. Perhaps this was her chance to do something right for once.

Smudge made to jump from the last rung of the ladder, but her foot caught in a vine and she landed face down in the bushes. The monkey, used to Smudge's clumsily executed midnight excursions round Littlefern Island when she was supposed to be asleep, didn't peer over the edge of the hammock just yet. And so, unnoticed, Smudge hurried through the undergrowth, crossed the sandy beach, then tiptoed over the wooden walkway towards Wildhorn.

She paused when she came to the cliffs encircling the island and peered round them into the bay. The elves' ship, **Dragonclaw**, was one of the nearest dhows, just a stone's throw from where she stood now and moored to a pier leading out from the beach. It was lit by lanterns and Smudge could see the Lofty Husks clustered at the bow. She stalled a moment longer. Was she really just going to stride aboard and start poking her nose into the elves' plans? Back in her hammock it had seemed like a good idea to let them know what she'd seen, but now, listening to Greyhobble's words, Smudge couldn't help feeling that this situation was far bigger than she was.

'An evil has risen from Everdark. Nothing

like this has ever happened before so we cannot know how much time we have before the magic that protects the Unmapped Kingdoms disappears, but, without a phoenix, my guess is that we don't have long.' Greyhobble paused. 'You all heard the greed and power in that creature's cry. It sounded hungry and, if it's out to steal Crackledawn's magic, we must act fast.'

He lowered his voice. 'Without magic, our seas will dry up, our lands will shrivel and every last drop of sun-chatter we have will vanish. Rumblestar, Jungledrop and Silvercrag will suffer a similar fate – and, without our magic, the Faraway will once more become a series of dark, empty places, as they were before the first phoenix sent the deep magic out into the world.'

The other elves exchanged anxious whispers.

'We must capture this creature, whatever it takes,' Greyhobble continued.

'But ... but without knowing what it is,' Timberdust stammered, 'how can we brew the right enchantments to stop it? And we don't even know which direction it went – is it still here in Crackledawn or has it made its way to one of the other kingdoms?'

Smudge's heart quickened. Her suspicion had been right: the Lofty Husks hadn't noticed what she had. So here it was at last, an opening for her to do something right – to say that she had **seen** the creature, that she **knew** it was a large, winged beast and that it was heading towards Lonecrag! And suddenly she didn't feel quite so small and stupid – the elves needed to hear what she had to say!

She rushed round the cliffs on to the beach, but as she did so something caught her eye: something fine and glinting falling

27

from the sky beyond the bay. It was like rain, only there wasn't a single cloud in sight, and this strange substance looked black against the moonlight as it moved closer and closer to the elves' ship.

Smudge nipped behind a cluster of palm trees, watching as one by one the elves looked up at the sky. A look of horror washed over them as tiny droplets fell over the bow of the boat leaving stains as dark as oil.

'Nightdaggers!' Greyhobble cried, rushing towards a large silver bell hanging from the rigging. 'Sound the alarm for the Unmappers! The creature is most definitely still in Crackledawn!'

Chapter 2

Smudge huddled behind the palm trees, too terrified to move. Although she couldn't always remember what she'd learned in class, she knew about dark magic. Every Unmapper did. Nightdaggers could turn you into a shadow, then hold you still, and the curse could only be lifted if the one who had conjured the dark magic in the first place undid it – or was stripped of their power.

Smudge's insides clenched as she stared at the scene aboard **Dragonclaw.** Greyhobble hadn't made it to the alarm

bell in time. Nor had any of the other elves
for that matter because the Nightdaggers
were falling too fast and Smudge could
only watch, shaking, as the rulers of her
kingdom faded – first their cloaks, then
their wrinkled skin and white hair – until
all that was left were a dozen shadows
clustered round a silent bell.

Pushing down her fear, Smudge
scrambled back over the sand. She had
to make it to Littlefern Island to warn
everyone. 'Wake up!' she screamed.
'**Wake up!**'

But the Nightdaggers were drawing back
from **Dragonclaw** now and spreading out
over the islands. Smudge started down the
walkway towards Littlefern only to realise
that the cursed rain was gathering above
it so she doubled back on herself and
ducked inside a small cave at the foot of
the cliffs.

'No,' Smudge breathed. 'No, no, no!'

But the Nightdaggers drummed on. Smudge's head spun. Had the curse been sent by the creature to stop those in Crackledawn who might try to come after it? Smudge watched as the Nightdaggers moved away from the islands and drifted out to sea, as silently as they had come. Then, when she was sure that the last of them had vanished from sight, she scampered out from her cave, ran across the walkway and peered up at the hammocks strung between the palm trees on Littlefern Island.

Shadows. In all of them. Dark, mute shapes where Unmappers should have been. Smudge scurried up the rope ladder to her own hammock, but there was no sign at all of the white-nosed monkey. She knew that magical beasts were immune to many of the curses that could harm Unmappers, so she hoped that meant the monkey was all right, but she couldn't help feeling that he could have at least stayed to check she was okay. It wasn't as if they were friends, though Smudge **had** secretly entertained the idea that he might become a companion of sorts when the Lofty Husks presented him to her at the beginning of the year.

Every first-former had been given an enchanted gift to mark the start of their formal lessons: Amira had received a telescope that whispered the names of the stars as you looked at them; Jago had been given a cutlass with a jewel in the hilt that glowed if danger was nearby; and Zeb got a pebble that predicted the weather. But Smudge had ended up with a white-nosed monkey that did nothing but follow her around in a grump. The elves had insisted the creature had an enchanted element, like all the other gifts, and Smudge had hoped that perhaps the monkey might speak or tell her future or produce something exciting from the impractically long suitcase he had arrived with. But he did nothing of the sort and seemed to be slightly cross with Smudge from the moment they met. Even so, she would've welcomed his company now.

Smudge climbed down once again and ran across the walkways between the other islands – Sandshell, Oldbark, Longvine, Driftwood – in case another Unmapper had escaped the Nightdaggers. But it was the same everywhere. Hammocks full of shadows.

'Somebody?' Smudge cried. 'Anybody!'

But nobody else, it seemed, had been somewhere they weren't meant to be that night. And, with a growing sense of dread, Smudge walked back to the bay and slumped down on to the sand in front of **Dragonclaw**. She had felt lonely for most of her life, but that was nothing compared to knowing that she was the **only** Unmapper not held by the Nightdaggers, a curse that had come in from the very direction the creature she had spotted had flown off towards.

She thought back to the ancient decrees and warnings that held her world and the Faraway together. But without a new phoenix rising how would the magic in her kingdom last? And how could they promise to pass it on to the Faraway if it wasn't here in the first place? Smudge tried to imagine Crackledawn without its magic – without the velvet sloths and glass-beaked toucans on Littlefern Island and without the whispers, giggles, hiccups and melodies that made watching a sunrise or a sunset feel like hearing a ninety-piece orchestra if you listened carefully. All that wonder, all that magic – gone; the Faraway plunged into darkness again.

Smudge let the horror of her thoughts sink inside her. Why hadn't the phoenix risen? What kind of creature had flown across the moon in its place? And who would capture it now the elves were bound by Nightdaggers? Would the Lofty Husks from other kingdoms work out a way to cross over into Crackledawn and rescue it? Or were they, too, enduring a similar fate?

Smudge swallowed back her tears. And it was then that the rock goblins inched out of their burrows. Smudge watched them whispering to one another on the beach. Several magical creatures lived alongside the Unmappers in Crackledawn – like the sand sprites, water pixies and cockle imps who spent their days frolicking in the shallows and eating puddleberries – but the rock goblins were the only ones who could talk. They kept to themselves, though, only ever speaking to Unmappers when brewing and selling Swigs, exotic fruit juices that made your bottom wiggle, in the Cheeky Urchin.

But the goblins didn't slope off into their burrows on seeing Smudge. Instead, they hobbled closer in their seaweed waistcoats and palm-leaf shorts until they were surrounding her. They were much smaller than her, but what they lacked in height they made up for in noses, which were so very bulbous it was surprising any of them could see where they were going.

'It's up to you to save the kingdom!' one goblin squeaked.

'Crackledawn needs you!' another piped up.

'You're the only hope!' a third squealed.

'Please can everyone stop shouting!' a fourth goblin, with a nose the size and shape of a very large potato, cried. She straightened her waistcoat and looked down at Smudge. 'You're pretty young to have been left in charge, aren't you?'

Smudge choked. '**Me?** Oh no. I'm here by accident. I'm not in charge!' She looked at the shadows frozen round the alarm bell on **Dragonclaw** and welled up again. 'I don't think anyone is any more ...'

The goblins dissolved into a frenzy of sobbing – all except the potato-nosed goblin who leaned closer to Smudge and said, in a whisper, 'Please don't **ever** say that again. Rock goblins fall apart under sloppy management.' She picked up a piece of driftwood and rapped Smudge on the knuckles with it. 'So keep it together and tell us what on earth you were doing out of bed tonight and how you are going to single-handedly save Crackledawn and the rest of the Unmapped Kingdoms from disaster?'

Smudge gulped. 'I ... I saw something earlier when we were waiting for the Rising,' she stammered. 'Something large and winged and terrible and it was flying towards Lonecrag, so I got out of my hammock—'

'Then what on earth are you doing chit-chatting with me here now?' the goblin cried. 'If you know that an evil creature is heading towards Lonecrag, why aren't you captaining a ship in pursuit of it?'

Smudge winced. 'I don't know how to steer one. Not properly anyway.'

The goblin waved her hand. 'Nonsense. What did you score in your Sunraiding tests?'

Smudge reddened. 'Um—'

The goblin rapped her on the knuckles again. 'Don't be modest – now's not the time.'

'I failed the tests,' Smudge mumbled.

'**Failed?**' the goblin hissed, trying not to let the rest of her kind overhear. She grimaced, then she hauled Smudge up and marched her past **Dragonclaw** and on to the second pier until she was standing before the ring of boats moored there. 'Pick a boat – any boat.'

Smudge backed away from the edge

of the pier, the steering incident still fresh in her mind. Besides, Unmappers weren't suppose to board dhows without being in possession of a watergum, the magical sweet which gave you gills to breathe underwater while diving for sun-chatter or acted as a safeguard against drowning if the seas got rough. But the goblin pushed her forward again regardless.

'A bit of pre-voyage nerves never hurt anyone,' she said. 'Now choose a boat.'

'But even if I do try to sail after the creature – which will be a disaster, by the way – what about the sun scrolls? How will the Faraway get sunlight if no one's writing the symphonies?'

'We'll do our best to take care of that while the other Unmappers are under the Nightdagger curse,' the goblin replied. 'You just focus on capturing the creature, demanding the release of the Unmappers and restoring order to the four kingdoms.'

Smudge gawped at her. 'But—'

The goblin turned to her friends and clicked her fingers. A bunch of bananas was bundled down the line of goblins towards her which she thrust at Smudge, saying: 'In case you get peckish on your trip' – before pushing her off the edge of the pier.

Smudge clattered into the hull of a boat and looked up see a crowd of goblins peering down at her over their noses.

'What did she say she scored in her tests?' one squeaked.

'Full marks,' the potato-nosed goblin replied, patting her friend on the back. She shot Smudge one last look over her shoulder as she hurried away. 'Try your utmost not to mess all this up, please – a change in management here in the Unmapped Kingdoms would be most distressing for us goblins and, though we're happy to help in the short term, we like an easy life, so we don't want to be left with the responsibility of writing the sun scrolls forever.'

Smudge didn't have the heart to tell her that there wouldn't **be** any Unmapped Kingdoms if the creature wasn't stopped, so she just smiled weakly until the rock goblins left and once again she was alone. She looked the boat up and down and then frowned. She recognised this boat. It was **The Coddiwomple**. The little dhow that had once belonged to the legendary Sunraider, Nefarious Flood, Smudge's all-time hero and the only person brave enough to have sailed beyond the Northswirl. She didn't remember much from her lessons in the Warren, but she remembered almost everything about Nefarious Flood because it wasn't really his sunraiding that people talked of but his adventures – his explorations in far-off places – and these were very much the sort of things that interested Smudge.

For a brief moment, Smudge considered Nefarious' fate: 'sailed beyond the Northswirl,' Crumpet had told her, 'and promptly drowned.'

His ship had been found adrift almost twenty years ago now – and it was only from his diaries on-board that anyone knew Nefarious had made it past the Northswirl because his body had never been found. The Lofty Husks had moored his boat here to remind Unmappers of the dangers of going beyond the Northswirl.

Smudge ran a hand over the dhow's hull. Even though the wooden sunshade erected over the stern had been battered by storms, the handle of the sunraiding net was chipped, the lantern hanging from the bow had a missing pane of glass and there were barnacles covering the benches, there was still something magical about the boat.

She imagined Nefarious Flood climbing aboard and sailing beyond the Northswirl.

How brave he must have been to venture out into the unknown! And, though Smudge still felt horribly, horribly out of her depth, she knew that now was not the time to let her fears get in the way of doing the right thing.

She stood up, eyes glittering. 'I might be a little bit useless,' she muttered, 'but I'm not a coward!'

Chapter 3

Smudge busied herself with the sail while,
unbeknown to her, the white-nosed monkey
watched from behind the cluster of palm
trees on the shore, holding a suitcase
in one hand and a trilby in the other. It
did seem to him that this under-aged,
underqualified and deeply underwhelming
eleven-year-old was indeed about to
embark on her first solo voyage – and that
was just as well because he had waited an
awfully long time for this. He hurried across
the beach towards the pier.

Meanwhile, Smudge eyed the

dragonhide sail. It was rolled up, but as soon as she placed a hand on the mast she felt the boat's magic shiver through her. She untied the sail and as it unfurled – a brilliant, shimmering gold sheet of leather covered in black-ink scribbles – she gasped. Because these were the destinations Nefarious Flood had visited on his last voyage.

'**The Gaping Gulf, Endless Falls, Ghostwreck** ...' Smudge murmured. But when she came to the name in the middle of the sail her toes began to tingle. '**The Northswirl.**'

Smudge ducked beneath the wooden canopy at the stern of the boat, opened a rusty trunk beneath it and rummaged through the contents. No watergums, annoyingly, but there was a penknife, several battered books – **An Insider's Guide to Catching Sun-chatter** by Peregrine Fingertwitch, **A Sunsmith's Manual** (includes tips on blending magical ink and writing memorable symphonies) by Augusta Prattle, **Where to Glimpse a Sea Dragon** by Algernon de Peep – a feather quill and an inkpot filled with black dye.

Smudge breathed a sigh of relief. 'Just enough squid ink left for **my** voyage.'

Then she thought of what might lie ahead – terrifying monsters, storms she couldn't tame, the creature itself in all its horror – and suddenly Smudge felt a flood of longing for a companion, for someone who might stop her legs wobbling and her heart hammering.

She took a deep breath, dipped her quill into the ink and, resigning herself to the fact that she was well and truly alone, she lifted the nib to an empty space on the sail. A word appeared by Smudge's hand, in black swirled lettering.

Destination:

Smudge scribbled her answer opposite.

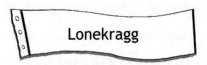

Lonekragg

A second passed, Smudge's writing
disappeared then the word 'autocorrect'
flashed in its place before vanishing and
leaving the spellchecked version of the
destination Smudge had intended.

Lonecrag

Smudge blushed. But the boat didn't seem
to mind that she couldn't spell because
now two more words appeared that
required an answer.

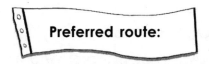

Preferred route:

Smudge considered this, then wrote:

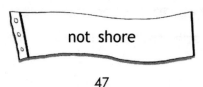

not shore

The spellcheck did a little more jiggling,
then asked for the final piece of information.

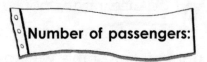

Number of passengers:

Smudge wrote her response as neatly as
possible (which wasn't very neat at all):

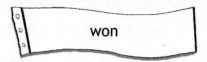

won

Predictably, the spellcheck flashed again,
but, rather more unpredictably, the words
on the sail now read:

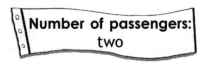

Number of passengers:
two

Smudge blinked. **Two?**

She glanced at the pier and jumped.
There was the white-nosed monkey
standing beside the boat, a trilby on his
head, his suitcase by his side.

'I thought you'd run off when the Nightdaggers came,' she said, 'but you're still here! And actually that's not such a bad thing because I think this might all go a bit better if I've got some company, even if it is in the form of a monkey who's never smiled.'

'If we are going to attempt this voyage together,' the monkey replied tartly, 'it would be far more agreeable if you would address me by my proper name.'

Smudge's mouth fell open because never, in all the time she had known the monkey, had she ever heard him speak. 'You – you can **talk**?'

'Of course I can talk.' The monkey lifted his leather suitcase and dropped it into the boat. 'It's just that up until now you have neither said nor done anything of interest, so I would only have been wasting my breath by speaking to you.'

He hopped aboard and sat cross-legged

on the bench opposite Smudge. The long grey hairs hanging from his cheeks twitched. 'But now I am ready for a conversation.'

'So your voice is your enchanted element?' Smudge murmured. 'I never knew!'

'My voice **and** my loyalty to you.' He sniffed. 'White-nosed monkeys are usually solitary animals, but, since the elves cast their enchantment over me, I have been obliged to traipse around after you.'

'And you have a name, you said?'

The monkey adjusted his trilby. 'My name is Bartholomew.'

Smudge considered this. 'Can I call you Bart for short? It's a bit of a mouthful otherwise.'

The monkey raised an eyebrow. 'Absolutely not. If there is one thing I cannot abide, it's nicknames. They are detestably common.' He poked Smudge in the back. 'I also loathe sloppy posture. If people were to face each day with a straight spine, they would accomplish a great deal more.'

Bartholomew leaned over the boat and untied the mooring rope. 'Well, are we setting sail or are we just going to sit here until whatever it was that rose from Everdark comes back and eats us?'

Smudge stood up. 'Right. Yes.' She placed a palm on either side of the dragonhide sail – the final touch needed for the boat to work its magic and carry its passengers, however weak or non-existent the wind was, to their selected destination. She looked shyly at Bartholomew. 'You're really coming with me?' she whispered. 'It's just that I've always thought you hated danger and risks and, well, anything at all that didn't involve sleeping or drinking tea. You always looked so unimpressed whenever I got into any kind of trouble.'

'I do hate danger,' the monkey replied. 'And risks. But last year I turned sixty-five – I know, you don't have to say it, Smudge, I don't look a day over thirty – and I was all set for a glorious retirement, but then, on a most uncharacteristic whim, I ended up offering my services to the Lofty Husks. I wanted to do my bit for Crackledawn before I took a long-earned rest, you know – it's been home to me and my ancestors for a great many years now. But, I must admit, I had rather thought a spot of cooking aboard **Dragonclaw** or a stint volunteering in the Den might have suited me better than being cast in an enchantment and given to you.'

Bartholomew steadied himself on the bench as the boat inched away from the pier.

'I may have gained a voice out of all this,' he went on, 'but, what with tramping around after you as you dilly-dally your way through life, my hopes of a restful retirement now seem depressingly far away. But –' he nibbled at his fingers as the boat wove its way between the walkways and drifted, despite the lack of wind, out to sea – 'now that the end of Crackledawn seems nigh and I see you're finally doing something sensible – running **away** from danger instead of **into** it – I thought I'd hop aboard.'

Smudge was starting to feel a little uneasy. 'Where exactly do you think we're going, Bartholomew?'

The monkey smiled wistfully. 'Somewhere beyond Crackledawn and all this nasty dark magic – somewhere wonderfully beautiful where I can retire.'

Smudge grimaced out to sea, but Bartholomew continued to chatter away.

'You see, when the elves gave me this position, they read my future in the stars. They said that one day you would sail me somewhere glorious – they didn't say when or where – and to be honest I rather thought it would be a little later in your Sunraiding career. But I've seen all your sketches of the lands beyond Crackledawn and here we are, sailing out to one of them now!'

Smudge wanted to say that those lands were places conjured from her imagination and that she had no idea **what** lay past Crackledawn or if she'd even be able to cross over into another land, but Bartholomew looked so happy that she didn't want to disappoint him.

Smudge glanced at the suitcase under the bench. 'What's in there?'

'My Uncle Jeremy's golf clubs,' Bartholomew replied. 'Retirement wouldn't be complete without them.' He rubbed his hands together. 'So, what irresistibly relaxing destination are we off to then?'

Smudge kept her eyes firmly on the sea. 'Lonecrag.'

Chapter 4

Bartholomew toppled backwards off the bench, then reappeared, seconds later, clutching his trilby. 'Lonecrag! That's deep-water territory where all those oversized eels splash about! In case you didn't know, white-nosed monkeys **loathe** deep water.' He shuddered. 'How on earth am I meant to relax alongside ogre eels and fire krakens? No, that won't do at all.'

Smudge turned to face him. 'We have to go to Lonecrag, Bartholomew – to save Crackledawn.'

The monkey seized his tail and held it

close. 'You mean to say that you're not running away?'

Smudge shook her head. 'I saw a winged creature after that terrible screech tonight and I watched it head out towards Lonecrag. I think it sent the Nightdaggers to curse Crackledawn and stall the Lofty Husks. So, now I'm going to trap the creature in a sunraiding net and force it to release the Unmappers. Then the elves will be free and once they get rid of the creature everything will go back to normal.'

Bartholomew gawped at Smudge. '**What?** But you're still just beginning your studies and, let's be honest, you're not exactly a star pupil. A sunraiding net might have magical properties, but how on earth do you think **you're** going to trap the creature that has already cursed every Unmapper in Crackledawn?'

'Every Unmapper except me,' Smudge said quietly.

Bartholomew picked up the sunraiding net. The handle was chipped and riddled with woodworm and the net itself was only the size of a dinner plate. But these nets could grow to fifty times their original size to accommodate vast hauls of sun-chatter and, if a Sunraider uttered the right spell, the rope that made up the net could bind its contents impossibly tight. Even so, Bartholomew didn't look convinced. 'I am **not** sure about this. Not sure at all.'

Smudge took a deep breath. 'Neither am I. In fact, the thought of facing the creature makes me feel completely terrified. But I can't just give up on Crackledawn and ... and I can't just give up on myself.' She glanced up at the velvet sky. 'I've always had a feeling inside me – a fierce little niggle – that I was born to do something different from everybody else, something extraordinary perhaps.' She put a hand on her chest. 'And I can feel that niggle in here right now.'

'Probably indigestion,' Bartholomew sniffed. 'That episode with the Nightdaggers would've been enough to rock the strongest of constitutions.'

Smudge ignored him. 'What if I'm right? What if the extraordinary thing I'm meant to do is save Crackledawn?'

Bartholomew sighed. 'It won't be like trapping sun-chatter, if that's what you're thinking.'

Smudge glanced at the lantern on the bow of the boat, which was now glowing gold against the night. She peered over the edge of the dhow and, though the sea was dark, now and again she caught a glimpse of the sun-chatter glittering on the ocean floor. The rest of her class would have known exactly what sounds they were, even without leaning closer to hear the sun-chatter whispering through the water, but Smudge was useless at identifying sun-chatter just through its whereabouts. She could never remember whether it was hiccups that lay just beyond Wildhorn or giggles that clung like barnacles to the rocks lining reefs further out or the other way around.

The Coddiwomple pushed on through the water, leaving Wildhorn far behind. Smudge sat down opposite Bartholomew. 'Once I've trapped this creature, I promise I'll swing by a peaceful island – maybe Turtle Shallows or Goldshell Cove – and drop you and your golf clubs off.'

Bartholomew huffed. 'And may I ask what provisions you have brought for us should we get waylaid on our little jaunt?'

Smudge's face lit up. 'Bananas. A whole bunch.'

Bartholomew threw her a withering look. 'We're off in pursuit of a creature whose cry made even Greyhobble's voice tremble

and we are armed with nothing but a
bunch of bananas?'

Smudge blushed – perhaps a little more
forward planning would have been helpful –
but the adventure had sort of started
without warning. Bartholomew sighed as he
flicked open the catches on his suitcase,
nudged the golf clubs aside and drew
out two china cups, a teapot and some
jungleleaf tea bags. Smudge noticed he'd
even packed a water purifier so that they
could make the tea using salt water.

'All I can say is thank goodness for
Great-aunt Mildred's tea set. **And** I brought
the leftover muffins we shared for supper
earlier, as well as a change of clothes
for you –' he reached over the side of
the boat and dunked the purifier into the
water – 'so, when we are held captive by
some ghastly sea creature, at least we will
not starve or look dishevelled during the
ordeal.'

They sipped their tea as the boat sailed on and on over the sleeping ocean and, though the prospect of accosting the creature – whatever it was – sent shivers down Smudge's spine, she did feel a tiny bit hopeful about the journey. Because there were no rules now – no blueprint for how things should be done. This was **her** voyage and, provided that she and Bartholomew didn't throttle each other en route, she was in with a chance of leaving her mark on the world at last.

After draining her tea, Smudge climbed up on to the roof of the canopy and cuddled up in the dusty blankets there. Bartholomew insisted he wasn't tired and, once he had scooped up the old coconut shells heaped in the bottom of the boat, he began thwacking them off the roof of the canopy with his golf club.

'Might as well get a bit of practice in,'

he muttered. 'My swing could do with some tweaking.'

But, when Bartholomew was sure that Smudge was asleep, he laid down his golf club, pulled the blankets up over the girl's shoulders and brushed the hair from her face. He rolled his eyes at his sentimentality. White-nosed monkeys were meant to be moody and aloof. Having complicated emotions and – worse still – expressing them was not at all the done thing.

Bartholomew sighed. The elves' enchantment really was a tricky thing. And now it made even going to sleep irritatingly problematic because, whether he liked it or not, he felt protective of Smudge. And that was all well and good back on Wildhorn, but out here, miles from home and from the wisdom of the Lofty Husks, it would be another matter entirely.

Chapter 5

'Sit up straight,' Bartholomew barked.

They were on top of the canopy of the dhow, eating muffins and sailing into the most splendid sunrise Smudge had ever seen. The wind had picked up, jostling the bronze-backed seagulls circling the mast and gusting against the dragonhide sail. Smudge breathed in the salt-filled air and for the briefest of moments she forgot that the existence of her kingdom was hanging by a thread and instead simply listened to the sun-chatter humming below the boat – a melody so sweet and pure it could have been made from honey.

Then Smudge's ears hooked on another sound and she clutched Bartholomew's arm. 'Listen ...'

It was a rumbling sort of purr that was almost a growl – and it was coming from the dark stack of rocks jutting out of the sea in the shape of a witch's hat, a few miles ahead.

'Lonecrag,' Smudge whispered and she shrank into her tunic. These were dangerous waters, out of bounds to unqualified Sunraiders, but here she was, sailing into the midst of them. A shiver crawled through her as she remembered the story of the kraken that had brought down three dhows with a single tentacle last year. Could she really be a match for such terrible beasts? Then she thought of the rock goblins back at Wildhorn beavering away in the Den. They were looking to her to capture the creature; she couldn't back out now, even though her heart was racing and her limbs were stiff with fear.

'My guess is that it's the creature making that noise,' Smudge whispered to Bartholomew.

The white-nosed monkey nodded. 'I believe ogre eels groan and fire krakens roar, so this could well be whatever you saw last night.'

Smudge slipped down from the canopy, picked up the sunraiding net, then handed the penknife to Bartholomew. 'Once we're close enough, I'll swipe at the creature with the net then, while you scribble Wildhorn on to the sail so the dhow is prepared to leave immediately, I'll perform the rope-locking spell to hold the creature in the net until we get back to **Dragonclaw**.'

Bartholomew shifted. 'You mean the spell that you attempted last week only it backfired and turned Crumpet's ears blue?'

Smudge tried not to think about that particular accident, but instead focused on the words she would have to say if she snared the creature in her net.

Bartholomew held up the penknife. 'Remind me why I've got this?'

'Backup.'

The monkey swallowed.

They sailed on silently. There were no seagulls in these parts and the marble-eyed dolphins that had been following them were now nowhere to be seen. But, more worryingly, Smudge noticed that the lantern at the bow was glowing far less frequently. Was the sun-chatter already starting to disappear because of the failed Rising? How long did they have before the magic of the phoenix ran out completely?

Smudge glanced over the edge of the

66

dhow and blinked. 'The water,' she hissed, 'it's black!'

The monkey nodded. 'Seawater can change colour depending on the types of creatures that swim in it. Silver for the silver whales – naturally – and green for sirens.'

'What makes it black?'

Bartholomew grimaced. 'Ogre eels and fire krakens, I presume ...'

Smudge edged closer to the monkey as the boat sailed on towards the rocks. They were slippery black and draped in seaweed and, though both Smudge and Bartholomew could still hear the strange purring, they couldn't see whether this was coming from a winged creature yet.

'What ... whatever is making that noise must be on the other side of the rock,' Smudge stammered.

Bartholomew was too frightened to reply, so Smudge pulled gently on the sail rope and the boat slowed until just the motion of the waves inched it forward. Smudge's mind reeled with what the creature might look like – a dragon with claws the size of swords, a hippogriff with a razor-sharp beak – and she felt an overwhelming urge to turn back for Wildhorn. But then the boat edged on a little more and an unexpected sight came into view.

Crouched at the base of the rocks by the water was a woman. At least, Smudge supposed it was a woman, though it was hard to tell because she was bald and her whole body was covered in a layer of puckered grey skin – like that of a plucked bird – and instead of feet she had talons. But there was something unmistakably female about the way she swished the feather cloak back and forth in the water before her and the way she purred to herself as she did so. Smudge and Bartholomew peered closer. Were those **wings** the woman was dipping into the

sea? And, if so, could this be the creature
Smudge had seen last night? But what kind
of creature was part bird, part woman?

'Thank you, fire kraken, for gifting me
your dark magic,' the woman crooned.
'Wings are power for a harpy and until
I am strong enough to begin my rule in
earnest I must look to loyal subjects, like
yourself, to sustain mine.'

Smudge tensed. **A harpy?** She couldn't
remember Crumpet ever speaking of
harpies and, while the creature before
her now didn't look like much, there was
something about her voice, as if it had
been chipped out of ice. Smudge leaned
out of the boat and caught a horrifying
glimpse of a large suckered tentacle before
it sank back into the sea.

'I will reward you soon for lending me
your strength,' the harpy called after the
fire kraken.

Smudge and Bartholomew watched,

transfixed, as the harpy lifted her wings out of the sea. The feathers spread out like a cloak and they were blacker than midnight and shining like oil, but it was only when Smudge saw the skull fixed in between where the wings parted that she realised the full extent of the evil before her.

The skull was long and narrow with a curved beak, and Smudge recognised it immediately from the sketches in her schoolbooks. She felt suddenly sick to her core. That was the skull of a phoenix and this hideous harpy was now slipping it over her head as casually as one might don a hat. Had the old phoenix died after five hundred years only for **this** to rise from the ashes to take its place?

'We need to ambush her before she takes flight,' Smudge whispered as the harpy threaded her spindly fingers through the hooks at the tips of her wings and the feathers spilled over her arms.

But, just as Bartholomew was drawing breath to reply, the harpy looked up and, though the skull masked her features, from the chill that slipped through her skin Smudge could tell that the harpy was looking right at them.

'Abort the mission!' Bartholomew cried, yanking on the sail rope to pull the boat away from the rocks. 'Retreat!'

But Smudge hadn't come all this way to flee. And, as the creature scuttled up the tower of rocks like an enormous beetle, the girl tightened her shaking hands round the sunraiding net, then pointed it in the direction of the rocks. Instantly, the net stretched, but the harpy launched into the sky and let out a terrifying screech.

Smudge stumbled into the bench as she tried to follow the harpy's movements with her net.

'Now is **not** the time to be clumsy, Smudge!' Bartholomew yelled. 'Catch the harpy in that net, then utter the rope-locking spell – fast!'

The harpy dipped her skull hood and plunged towards the boat. As she drew close, Smudge swiped at her with the net but the harpy was stronger than Smudge had anticipated and she smacked Smudge to the ground, then hurtled on by. Again the harpy rose into the air and again she dived, but Smudge was on her feet now, brandishing the net, her eyes wide with fear. This time when the harpy tore close Smudge ducked just in time, then whirled round to try and snag the creature's wings. But the harpy shrieked and swerved past the boat at the very last moment.

Bartholomew was surprised to see that although there didn't seem much of a rhythm to Smudge's fight or, in fact, much accuracy, there was a dogged sort of determination, an outright refusal to give up – and it spurred the monkey to act.

Down the harpy came again, too fast
for Smudge to angle her net in the right
direction, but that didn't matter because
Bartholomew flung his penknife towards the
creature and, on seeing the glint of metal
careering towards her, the harpy jerked to
the side, batting the knife back into the
boat, then flew on past.

Smudge scampered up on to the
canopy and, while Bartholomew stood at
the bow, screaming all sorts of words a
monkey should never repeat, she thrust
her net into the harpy's flight. The creature
thundered into it and the force brought
both her and Smudge tumbling down
into the boat. The harpy screeched and
thrashed her wings, but undeterred Smudge
began to recite the rope-locking spell:

'Rope of mine please hold fast
Do not break until I ... I ...'

Her mind went blank and before she could remember the final word – **'ask'** – the harpy burst free, snapping the net in two. Bartholomew hurled his penknife as the harpy launched into the sky but it overshot and landed in the sea.

Smudge's head spun with panic. The net was in pieces and their only weapon was gone. In a matter of moments, the harpy could kill her and Bartholomew – and then who would stop this creature destroying the Unmapped Kingdoms? Who would be left to fight the dark magic? The truth crowded in on Smudge: this creature was too much for her and Bartholomew. It was madness thinking they could take a harpy on ...

'Watch out!' Bartholomew screamed as the harpy plummeted towards the boat.

Smudge jerked the mast so that the dhow turned, but, just before it did, the harpy's talons raked through the dragonhide sail, leaving a gash right down the middle. Smudge froze. **The Coddiwomple**'s sail was torn. And now the one option still open to them – to flee – had gone.

Chapter 6

Bartholomew picked up the broken net as the harpy rose to make another dive. But the rope was well and truly torn and the handle had been smashed. 'Quick!' he yelled. 'Open the trapdoor into the hull!'

Smudge jumped over the benches towards the stern. Every dhow had about a metre or two of space in the hull, which you could access through a trapdoor and hide in during stormy weather. So she scrambled towards the square of wood amid the planks which had what looked like a handle indent in the middle and the word **'lift'** engraved onto it. Smudge pulled hard as the harpy shrieked and raced down towards them. But the trapdoor wouldn't budge.

Bartholomew ditched the net, flung himself towards the trapdoor and then, quite unexpectedly, he began to laugh. Not a nervous chuckle or a little chortle but loud, short bursts of hysterical giggling.

The harpy was only a few metres away now and Smudge braced herself for its grappling claws, but then Bartholomew grabbed her by the arm and yanked her through the trapdoor he had somehow managed to open. Smudge clattered down a flight of steps and looked up to see Bartholomew fastening a chain across the underside of the door. Above deck, the harpy beat its talons against the wood and thrashed with its mighty wings. But the trapdoor held fast. And, after a while, the

pummelling stopped and a grating voice
slipped through the cracks.

'Every phoenix, since the beginning
of time, has shared its magic with the
Unmapped Kingdoms and the Faraway.
But I, Morg, rose from the ashes of the last
phoenix with one aim: to take every scrap
of magic in these kingdoms for my own.
The Faraway will perish, but what will I care
when I have the Unmapped Kingdoms at
my disposal? I will command the sun to
blister and scorch, I will call on the rain to
unleash mighty storms and I will summon
the snow to cast the fiercest blizzards!
Under me, a new era will be born and I
will fill it with creatures conjured from dark
magic.

'You two may have escaped my
Nightdaggers, but know that I will brew
deadlier curses in Everdark, curses that will
knock the life out of you in seconds when
we cross paths again. Then I will fly on to

the other kingdoms and, once I have every Unmapper under my curse, I shall begin my rule. And there is no point trying to stop me because you cannot reach Everdark. No one has crossed the Northswirl and lived.'

There was a scuttling sound of claws over wood, followed by a whir of wings and then, finally, silence.

Bartholomew breathed out, then he looked at Smudge with an expression she couldn't quite put her finger on.

'You were,' the monkey reflected, 'not as disastrous as I thought you'd be out there.'

Smudge hung her head. 'I forgot the last word of the spell and then Morg snapped the net in half.'

Bartholomew shrugged. 'True – the incantation **was** a little sloppy. But you were brave, Smudge. Remarkably brave in fact. Of course, we'd be nowhere without my devilishly quick mind, but still, you surprised me.'

Smudge blushed. She couldn't remember ever receiving a compliment before and she wasn't entirely sure what the appropriate response was so she settled for humming. And although she doubted there was much hope of her and Bartholomew becoming close friends on the voyage – she was bound to mess things up for them both soon and their muddling along beside each other was only because the elves had entrusted the monkey with loyalty – it was at least reassuring to know that he thought her brave and that together they had managed to escape the harpy's clutches.

Smudge glanced up at the trapdoor. 'How on earth did you manage to open it? It was jammed shut when I tried.'

'It said **lift** on the handle,' Bartholomew explained. 'Laugh Intensely Five Times.' He pushed past Smudge and walked down the steps. 'I do wish you were just **slightly**

better at listening in class. Still, it could
have been worse. We could have had
a **pull** trapdoor – Pirouette Unbelievably
Ludicrously Loudly – and then we would
have been in all sorts of bother.'

Smudge, however, was no longer
listening to the monkey. They weren't in a
tiny space in the hull, as she had expected.
Now that she looked around properly, she
saw that the trapdoor had opened on to
a sweeping staircase that couldn't possibly
exist because everyone knew dhows were
only two metres deep, but somehow the
staircase was here all the same. It seemed
that Nefarious Flood's boat was imbued
with more magic than most.

Smudge made her way down the rest
of the stairs and found herself looking at a
secret cabin unlike anything she had ever
seen before. Glow-worm lanterns dangled
from the roof of what appeared to be a
study, the walls were covered in plaques

displaying the mounted tails of sea monsters that Nefarious had presumably slain and at the far end of the room was a mahogany desk covered with maps. An armchair plumped with cushions and raised on wooden crab legs had been pulled up to the desk and there were towers of leather-bound books surrounding it, as well as a row of shelves above filled with sketches of sea dragons, jars of multicoloured sand and messages rolled up in bottles.

Smudge's eyes shone as she took in the two little alcoves on either side of the study: a tiny kitchen on the left and a cubbyhole bedroom complete with a circular window looking out on the sea to the right.

'This is incredible ...' she breathed.

Bartholomew straightened the rug on the study floor, then recentred a cutlass hanging from the wall. 'Yes, this will do very nicely for our journey back to Wildhorn.'

Smudge looked up from studying a boomerang covered in merscales that she had spotted on top of a trunk. 'Back to Wildhorn?'

The monkey nodded. 'We're going into hiding – the caves there will be just the thing.'

'I don't think this is something you can hide from, Bartholomew. You heard what Morg said: she's planning to take every scrap of magic from the Unmapped Kingdoms.' Smudge drew herself up. 'Her curses will find us, however far inside a cave we hide, so we have to get to her before she gets to us. Because **this** is our chance to do something extraordinary – to save not just the Unmapped Kingdoms but the Faraway, too.'

Bartholomew took off his trilby and turned it over in his hands. 'Most people live ordinary lives, Smudge. And that's perfectly okay. We should head back to

Wildhorn and scour every book in the Warren until we find a way to wake the Lofty Husks. Then we can leave it to them to fix everything.'

Smudge shook her head. 'By now you should know that I'm not most people. My head is filled with **what ifs** and **just maybes**. So, what if the people who end up changing the world aren't always the ones that shine in class or come first in exams? What if, just maybe, it's about trying and hoping and never giving up, even when things look impossible?' She paused. 'We have to go on, Bartholomew, because the only thing a person needs to do something extraordinary is an opportunity. And **this** is ours.'

The monkey put his hands on his hips. 'And **how** exactly do you plan to stop this unreasonably aggressive harpy?'

'By being cunning,' Smudge replied, trying to sound brave, 'and also a little bit bold.'

'Says the girl who doesn't even know how to open an enchanted trapdoor.' Bartholomew slumped into the armchair. 'Go on then – what's your plan?'

Smudge narrowed her eyes. 'We know something we didn't know before: Morg's power lies in her wings. So ... we're going to set sail for Everdark and steal them.'

Bartholomew turned an odd shade of green. 'You mean to say that the next stop on the retirement cruise is –' he swallowed – **'the Northswirl**?'

Smudge nodded. 'I'm afraid so.' She glanced up at the trapdoor. 'I suggest you bring down Great-aunt Mildred's tea set. You look like you could do with a cuppa.'

Chapter 7

When Bartholomew had poured himself
a fourth cup of tea, Smudge figured his
nerves would probably have recovered
enough for them to start planning their
next step, so she began rummaging
through the drawers in the mahogany desk.
There was still no sign of any watergums,
which would've settled Bartholomew's
nerves a little at the prospect of stormy
seas ahead, but there were other things of
note.

'Found it!' Smudge held up a reel of
purple thread with a needle slotted into it.

'This I **do** remember from class: mersilk – perfect for repairing torn sails.'

She hurried up the steps, listening hard beneath the trapdoor for anything untoward, then, when she was satisfied, she climbed up on deck. She flinched as she took in the gashes Morg's talons had made in the dhow's wood and for a second she faltered. Could they really steal the wings of such a powerful creature? Then the niggle in her chest burned harder and, pushing down her doubts, she set to work on the sail and tried not to think of all the ogre eels and fire krakens that might be stirring beneath the boat.

Minutes later, the mersilk had worked its magic: the rip had vanished and the sail glinted gold in the midday sun. Smudge picked up the quill, dipped it in the squid ink, then raised her hand to the very corner of the sail, where there was still just enough room left to write.

Destination:

Smudge thought of the lands she'd imagined past the Northswirl. What mysterious beasts swam in those seas? Were there secret caves and hidden waterfalls? Magical reefs and undiscovered bays? And how far across those seas was Everdark? Smudge's mind wandered to her hero, Nefarious Flood, setting out in this very boat, for the exact same destination, and never coming back. She gripped her quill tighter. If Bartholomew sensed any doubts, he'd try again to persuade her to go back to Wildhorn – and that wasn't going to happen. She wrote quickly.

Northswurl

Once again, the sail autocorrected her spelling then, quite unexpectedly, there was a loud flap as the dragonhide shook itself against the ropes that bound it and small black scales appeared through the leather.

Bartholomew was up on deck in an instant. 'What was that noise? What have you broken?'

'Nothing – all I did was tell the boat where to go ...'

The sail was now covered in jet-black dragonscales, which glittered darkly in the sunlight. Then there was a clicking sound, like a light being turned on, and a turquoise flame flickered inside the lantern on the bow of the boat. This was no longer a radar for the vanishing sun-chatter, Smudge realised, this was a lamp to guide them through the Northswirl! A clanking sound echoed from the sides of the boat – like gears slotting into place – but strangely there was nothing to show for it afterwards.

Bartholomew raised an eyebrow. 'Looks like the boat is preparing for the Northswirl ...'

The dhow swung past Lonecrag, leaving the fire krakens and the ogre eels to their slumbers, and, with a sail full of wind and magic, it headed north through the winking waves. The sky was a deep blue, strewn with wisps of cloud, but the ocean seemed eerily quiet now that there was less sun-chatter buried in its depths.

Smudge hurried back down the steps, with Bartholomew following close behind, then she gobbled down a banana and settled herself in the armchair before the desk. She picked up the map in front of her. 'The Northswirl is marked,' she said to Bartholomew, who was grimacing at a bottle on the desk that was filled with green liquid and labelled **kraken blood**. 'But there's nothing beyond that – just blank parchment.'

Bartholomew groaned. 'So we're searching for a destination not even a celebrated Sunraider's map shows?'

'Let's focus on the Northswirl first then, because it'll take us most of today to reach it. They say the waves there are as big as houses and I bet the reason Nefarious Flood died is because he hoped that he could outride them. But that plan obviously didn't work. So, what if the answer is to simply worry about staying afloat rather than riding through the waves?' She scanned the cabin. 'Where do you think Nefarious would keep a lifebuoy?'

No sooner had the words popped out of her mouth than the armchair she was sitting in scuttled across the cabin on its crab claws and paused in front of a chest outside the kitchen.

'Well, I never!' Bartholomew cried, scampering after the chair. 'A genuine obligasaurus!'

'A **what**?'

Bartholomew ran a hand over the armchair. 'A distinctly elegant and terribly helpful style of furniture first introduced in the third century.' He smiled. 'My great-grandfather used to swear by them for improving posture, too, but I never thought I'd see one in my lifetime.' He glanced at the chest in front of them. 'Well, go on then – open up the chest. The obligasaurus didn't stop in front of it because it likes the view.'

Smudge heaved the chest open and there, inside, was a lifebuoy!

Bartholomew looked at the lifebuoy then up at Smudge. 'I fear we'll need a little more than that to keep us afloat in the Northswirl, but I shall leave you to your wayward thoughts while I take a much-needed siesta in the cubbyhole. All this adventuring is playing havoc with my nerves.'

Smudge sat back down in the armchair and tried to gather her thoughts. 'I need to think about this differently,' she murmured.

'With all the **what ifs** and the **just maybes** of the situation …'

She found the valve on the lifebuoy and undid it. The air hissed out and Smudge felt her pulse quicken. No Sunraider had ever dared tamper with a dhow's safety equipment and yet she **had** to come at things from a different angle if there was even the slightest hope of them crossing the Northswirl. She hurried back to the desk and eyed the glass bottles on the shelf above it. She squinted at the first – a bottle containing a navy blue liquid flecked with green glitter.

'Not siren tears,' she mumbled. 'They probably wouldn't work. But what about this?' She lifted up a stoppered bottle containing a liquid that looked like marbled gold then read the wording on the little tag tied round the cork. 'The breath of a sea dragon. That might just do it …'

She poured the liquid through the valve

of the lifebuoy, then she closed it up, tied the float to the bundle of rope also in the trunk, and sat back down in the obligasaurus, which had very conveniently parked itself before the desk again.

'Now something for the whirlpools because, if Crumpet's been telling the truth, they spin faster than tornadoes.' Smudge's mind raked over everything she'd been taught in class about navigating stormy seas until her mind was wandering freely. Then she looked down at the armchair. 'I need to find a pocket watch.'

The obligasaurus stayed where it was and Smudge frowned, then she opened the drawers of the desk in front of her. The first few she skipped past – nothing except old quills, notebooks and a few packs of cards – but eventually she found the pocket watch in a corner of the bottom drawer. It was still ticking, after all this time, and it even showed the correct time – half past three in the afternoon – so Smudge guessed that this was a magical pocket watch. And **they**, Crumpet had said, were capable of all sorts of things, not simply showing the time, if handled correctly.

Smudge pushed back the catch that held the glass face in place. 'No one's ever **said** this would work,' she murmured, lifting a jar of purple sand from the shelf above the desk and sprinkling a few grains over the clock face. 'But I don't see why not. It's sand from Turtle Shallows, after all ...'

Bartholomew's eyes flickered open from the cubbyhole then narrowed as they took in what Smudge was doing. The Sunraiders back at Wildhorn had never considered enclosing the multicoloured sand in a pocket watch – it was mostly just used by Unmappers as a decorative item. But perhaps Smudge was hoping she could use it in another way, only quite what Bartholomew had no idea. The monkey gave up trying to make sense of things and drifted off to sleep again and for that reason neither he nor Smudge noticed the giant eel slithering past the cubbyhole window.

And this creature wasn't just passing by. It had been following their every move since Morg had spoken to it back at Lonecrag.

Chapter 8

It turned out that there were supplies in the kitchen: a range of jungleleaf teas along with a few cans of beans that Smudge and Bartholomew wolfed down. Meanwhile, outside the cubbyhole window, the sea turned darker. The sun had already set and Smudge noticed that the creatures drifting past the glass were altogether stranger now: jellyfish with luminous tentacles that stretched the length of the boat, shoals of multicoloured fish that swam backwards instead of forwards and once, though it passed so quickly she couldn't be sure,

Smudge thought she saw the tail of a mermaid.

The waves were bigger in these parts, too, and **The Coddiwomple** was already tilting from side to side. The larger pieces of furniture had been nailed to the floorboards years ago, but Smudge and Bartholomew had bolted shut every cupboard, wardrobe and chest in the cabin in anticipation of what might lie ahead.

Smudge felt her skin prickle. They were nearing the Northswirl, the very place that had filled her dreams back on Littlefern Island. She had longed to see it – longed to cross it – but now that she was heading into its grasp she suddenly felt small and afraid.

'We must be close by now,' she whispered.

A wave shunted against the dhow, knocking a mounted hydra tail to the floor.

Bartholomew clutched the wall for support, but then another wave juddered the boat from the other side and a can of beans rolled across the rug.

'And this is only the beginning ...' Bartholomew moaned.

The waves roared above deck and the wind groaned. Smudge thought of Nefarious Flood steering towards the Northswirl all those years ago – had his heart been thundering against his ribcage, like Smudge's was now? Had the doubts whirling through her mind been whirling through his, too? Smudge steeled herself. She couldn't let her fear get the better of her, not when they were this close. So she wound the rope from the lifebuoy over her shoulder and headed towards the steps.

'You're sure we should be going up on deck in this?' Bartholomew asked as the dhow veered on its side, then thumped down on to the water.

Smudge felt for the watch in the pocket of her tunic. 'We can't just sit tight and hope for the best. We've got to be cunning, remember? We've got to outwit both the storm **and** the Northswirl.'

Bartholomew hugged his tail as a rumble of thunder passed over the boat. 'But I don't have the arms for swimming if it comes to that! And you don't have any experience – or perspective – or common sense!' he wailed. 'We don't even have any watergums – we could drown, Smudge!'

Smudge looked back at him. 'I'm scared, too, Bartholomew – but if we turn away from the Northswirl, like everyone else has done in the past, Morg will win. We've **got** to do things differently.'

She clambered up the stairs and pushed the trapdoor open. The rain gushed in, soaking her tunic and plastering her hair to her skin, and the wind howled louder. Smudge thrust her body out on to the deck and, behind her, the shaking monkey followed.

The night had closed in around them, but the lantern burned bright and Smudge gasped at the scene before her. The sea was a churning pit of waves and the sky blazed with lightning.

A wave arched over the boat, then thumped down, forcing Smudge and Bartholomew to their knees. They staggered up, coughing salt water, as the storm clouds bulged across the sky. But, despite the storm, **The Coddiwomple** continued to inch forward, its dragonhide sail seeming stronger and even more determined than ever as it carried the dhow closer and closer to the most enormous whirlpool Smudge had ever seen.

'We've got to cross **that**?' Bartholomew shrieked.

A peal of thunder tore across the sky and the rain fell harder.

'Whirlpools line the length of the Northswirl, remember?' Smudge yelled. 'We've got no choice but to sail over them!'

'We'll be sucked to our deaths!'

The boat moved nearer still and Smudge's heart clamoured as she took in the circle of spinning water before them. It was the size of a fairground wheel and at its centre was a gaping hole carved out by the fast-spinning water around it.

'Hold on!' Smudge cried as the boat entered the outskirts of the swirl and spun wildly.

Bartholomew clung to the side of the boat as Smudge set the lifebuoy down and rummaged in her pocket because her plan, their only hope of crossing this whirlpool, lay in the folds of her tunic. She drew her arm back, clutching the pocket watch in her shaking fist, then for a second she wavered. What if her idea didn't work? But the boat was spinning faster and faster and Smudge realised she didn't have time for doubt. She had to act. **Now**.

So, hoping hard, she hurled the pocket watch into the heart of the whirlpool.

Smudge held her breath and Bartholomew held his tail and the boat continued to spin. Then – miraculously – the whirlpool started to slow, to unravel almost, and, as the boat stopped turning, Smudge saw that the hole in the middle of the whirlpool had closed up. Either side of the dhow there were more giant whirlpools and above them the storm still raged, but the way ahead – the narrow passage of water cutting through the waves – was, all of a sudden, astonishingly calm.

'It worked!' Smudge gasped. 'My idea actually worked!'

Bartholomew blinked in amazement. 'But

I don't understand ... I'd heard that some pocket watches are magical – they last forever and can speed up journey times with the right ingredients scattered inside them – but how can they calm a sea?'

'We visited Turtle Shallows on a field trip once,' Smudge replied as the boat sailed through the channel, 'and the whole class was given a jar of multicoloured sand as a souvenir. I scattered mine below a palm tree on Littlefern Island, to see what happened, and all the animals, everything from the velvet sloth to the dancing parrot, moved far more slowly when they came into contact with the Turtle Shallows sand because of its magic. So I sort of figured – or hoped, I suppose – that if I combined the magical sand with a watch it might somehow slow time down rather than speeding it up.'

'And, by doing so, slow down the whirlpool!' Bartholomew laughed. 'Well done, Smudge!' And then he looked ahead and gulped. 'I hope you have something equally clever for **that**?'

Smudge followed his gaze and her mouth fell open. Some way ahead, and blocking their path completely, was a wave. Only this wave was nothing like any she'd seen before and it made the ones from the storm that still raged either side of them look tame. This was a single looming barrier of water that stretched the height of a church spire and, for some reason, it wasn't keeling over and breaking. It was heading straight for them.

'I ... I'm not sure my idea will work,' Smudge stammered. 'I didn't imagine waves could get that big!'

The storm inhaled and, in the face of this terrible wave, what magic the pocket watch had cast over the whirlpool now vanished. Suddenly water charged at the dhow again, hammering against the sail and knocking Smudge and Bartholomew to the deck. They hauled themselves up only to be flattened seconds later by another wave which tore the lantern from the bow and sent broken glass spinning through the air. The darkness advanced and the thunder bellowed.

'We could try sailing **through** the wave instead of **over** it!' Bartholomew shouted.

But then, as if the wave had heard the monkey, it began curling over at its peak. Smudge's eyes grew large as she realised that the foam tearing down towards them had sharpened into hundreds of spikes lit up by the flashes of lightning. Smudge screamed as she saw the base of the wave was also studded with spikes. The wave had transformed itself into a mouth with jagged teeth and they were sailing right inside it.

Smudge snatched up the lifebuoy. 'There's no point thinking of sailing through or over anything, Bartholomew!' she screamed. 'We just need to stay afloat if we want to survive!'

The boat shook violently as it crossed the teeth lining the bottom of the wave and Bartholomew made a beeline for the trapdoor. But Smudge was now shimmying up the mast with the lifebuoy, and – though the storm howled around her, the fanged wave loomed above the boat and Smudge's pulse raced – she tied the rope as tightly as she could round the top of the mast.

Then she jumped down, leaving the lifebuoy hanging up there, and hurtled towards the trapdoor, flinging herself inside just as the wave folded over the boat. The force of the blow not only knocked Smudge and Bartholomew down the steps but it turned the boat on its side. **The Coddiwomple** shunted downwards and though the dhow managed to flip itself upright again there was no mistaking what was happening.

The wave was dragging them down into the depths of the sea.

'We're ... we're sinking!' Smudge stammered, turning her terror-stricken face towards Bartholomew. 'There's no way the lifebuoy can keep us afloat now! I was mad to even think it could!'

Bartholomew clutched her hands as the boat drifted down. The cabin was a wreck of smashed furniture and shattered glass and there was water dripping through the trapdoor.

'You were right all along, Bartholomew,' Smudge sobbed. 'We should have turned back for Wildhorn when we had the chance and searched for a way to lift the curse on the Lofty Husks. But now,' she sniffed, 'we've failed Crackledawn, we've failed Rumblestar, Silvercrag and Jungledrop **and** we've failed the Faraway!' She clutched her head in despair.

The noise of the storm grew quieter as the boat sank further into the depths of the ocean, but Bartholomew's words were loud and clear. 'I might have doubted you at first, Smudge, but I should have had more faith. Most people spend their whole life never knowing the strength that lies inside them. They live timidly and are too scared to speak up or step out. But you're not afraid, Smudge. You dared to believe that you are capable of extraordinary, impossible things.'

A tear rolled down Smudge's cheek. 'But I was wrong, wasn't I?' The boat groaned under the weight of the sea.

Bartholomew squeezed Smudge's hands. It was only a little squeeze, but there was something about the way the monkey held her hands, his old paws wrapped firmly round her fingers. Smudge had never thought Bartholomew liked her, but as she looked into the monkey's eyes she now realised, for the first time, that they were big and kind and shining with loyalty.

'It isn't easy to believe in oneself,' Bartholomew said. 'In fact, sometimes it's easier to believe in things like dragons and witches, though they are rarely seen. But to know the quiet strength of your spirit – and to count on it in times like these – is to understand what it means to be truly brave.'

Smudge brushed the tears from her eyes.

'I underestimated you,' Bartholomew said, 'but I will never do so again. Because the strength inside you is iron-strong and, if you can find it again now, and hold it, just for a second, I believe things might turn out all right.'

Smudge watched the sea scroll past the cubbyhole window – down, down, down they went – but Bartholomew's words, so different from the sniggering of her classmates and the Lofty Husks' lectures, kindled something inside her. She took a long, deep breath and dared to believe in herself again. And, as she did so, a peculiar thing happened ...

The boat stopped sinking and began, very slowly, to drift upwards.

'What's – what's happening?' Smudge gasped.

Bartholomew smiled. 'I noticed the tag on the empty bottle on Nefarious' desk ... You filled the lifebuoy with a sea dragon's breath because you remembered that it's more powerful and more buoyant than ordinary air. But you forgot one thing.' The boat floated on up. 'A sea dragon's magic only works if the person in charge of it believes in themself as well as in the magic.'

Smudge hugged Bartholomew tight. 'Oh, clever old you for remembering! For telling me to hope!'

The monkey stiffened in her embrace and things became terribly awkward. 'Ahem, yes, very nice. Thank you.' He stood up and shook the water from his fur as the boat bounced up on to the surface of the waves. Then he turned a very serious face towards Smudge. 'If you breathe a word about that hug or my overly sentimental words earlier, I am afraid I shall have to disown you completely. I appear to have lost control of my emotions.' He picked up his trilby and put it on. 'And that will not do at all.'

Smudge grinned as she leaped up the steps, two at a time, and pushed the trapdoor open. The boat had taken a battering – there was water everywhere, the sail had almost completely come loose and the benches had splintered right through – but **The Coddiwomple** was still afloat and that in itself felt like a miracle. Smudge threw back her head and laughed.

Because she and Bartholomew had done it: they had crossed the Northswirl – and lived.

Chapter 9

Smudge leaned against the bow of the boat and peered through the dark. The sky was still full of clouds and the air was misty with drizzle, but the storm had passed and they were one step closer to Everdark and to finding out what else lay beyond the Northswirl.

Bartholomew emerged through the trapdoor and Smudge squinted harder into the gloom. 'It just looks like miles and miles of open sea around us ...'

The monkey ran his paws across the stern. 'That clanking noise we heard after

The Coddiwomple transformed its sail and altered its lantern ... I thought perhaps the boat might have had an extra weapon to help protect us, but I can't see anything different.'

The clanking noise had, as Bartholomew had guessed, been an extra weapon, but it was too dark for either he or Smudge to see the little slits on the railings through which thousands of merscales had poured when the fanged wave dragged them down. Because, unbeknown to those aboard the dhow, there had been a final threat readying to pounce in the Northswirl, and sensing it, **The Coddiwomple** had hurled the one thing capable of beating an ogre eel – merscales – out into the sea when the monster drew close. Now the eel lay stunned into a trance at the bottom of the ocean but even merscales cannot hold back evil forever. And it would have helped Bartholomew and Smudge immensely if they had known that by the next moonrise there would be a rampaging monster tailing their boat. For now, though, they sailed on unawares.

Bartholomew fumbled through the trunk under the canopy, then his face dropped. 'We forgot to take the quill and ink down into the cabin.' He looked up at Smudge. 'They're gone ... Tossed overboard by the storm.'

Smudge glanced nervously at the sail. 'How will we direct the ship without them?' She slumped against the side of the boat. They'd got this far – they'd achieved what no other Sunraider had – and yet now it seemed they were stuck! 'How could we have been so careless?' she muttered.

Bartholomew was silent for a moment, then he looked up at Smudge. 'I wonder,' he said thoughtfully. 'I just wonder ...'

He beckoned her back towards the trapdoor and Smudge followed him down inside the cabin, desperately hoping the monkey's hunch – whatever it was – was right. The obligasaurus was whizzing back and forth, straightening hydra tails and hauling up furniture. It had claws tucked under its armrests, as well as below the seat, it appeared, and these were working tirelessly to set the cabin right.

Bartholomew's face lit up. 'If the place is being given a spring clean, then I might well be able to find what I'm looking for.'

The obligasaurus seized a broom and began sweeping up the rogue sea-hoppers (miniature toads that could burp the alphabet backwards) that had escaped from a toppled fish tank.

Bartholomew hurried over to the desk and began rummaging through the papers the obligasaurus had stacked back on its surface.

Smudge frowned. 'What **are** you looking for?'

'This,' Bartholomew said. 'The map we consulted right at the beginning of our voyage. I think that it might be a mind map.'

'A mind map?' Smudge said gloomily. 'Crumpet gets us to do those for revision before exams – not that they helped me much – but mine looked nothing like this. And how is a mind map going to help us anyway?'

Bartholomew waved his hand dismissively. 'A real mind map is nothing like the kind of thing you came across in class.'

He unfolded it on the desk and Smudge did a double take. When they had last looked at the map, there had been nothing beyond the Northswirl but now, strewn across the parchment, were words written in swirling ink.

The land you seek is not so far.
Sail on beneath the northmost star.

In time you'll find the Fallen Crown
Unless, that is, you end up drowned.

'Not quite as upbeat as I would have
hoped,' Bartholomew reflected. 'But
constructive nonetheless.'

Smudge ran a finger over the words.
'How did you know that this was a mind
map and that it would tell us where
to go?'

'I didn't,' Bartholomew replied. 'But I
did wonder why there was such a large
blank space above the Northswirl. It just
seemed like something was missing and
I vaguely remember reading a book
once, a fascinating and reassuringly
in-depth exploration of Crackledawn's
history, which touched upon the degrees
of magic found in the kingdom. Slightly
Magical at the Sighing Caves, for example,
Intermittently Magical back at Lonecrag
and –' he looked Smudge squarely in the

eye – '**Highly** Magical at the Northswirl. So it stands to reason that only here would this map reveal the destinations pressing on our minds.'

Smudge looked round the cabin. The obligasaurus was taking a break in the corner and the whole place was sparklingly clean, but also, Smudge realised, ever so slightly different from how it had looked before, as if only now that they were past the Northswirl was the cabin revealing its Highly Magical belongings.

There was a little jar filled with what appeared to be foil-wrapped sweets on the desk, which definitely hadn't been there before, and, at the sight of them, Smudge cheered. 'Watergums!'

'What luck!' Bartholomew picked up the jar then frowned. 'But these look different from the ones in the Den ...'

Smudge read the label aloud:
'**Watergums – eat if beyond the Northswirl.**'

And then, in smaller letters below this:
'**Enables breathing underwater, of course, but also talking, singing, laughing, whistling and, if needs be, burping (one sweet lasts a lifetime but allow several hours for optimum effect).**'

Bartholomew frowned. 'Quite why we'd want to laugh underwater, I've no idea – there is nothing funny, to a white-nosed monkey, about being beneath the surface of the sea – but these, at least, are stronger than the watergums kept in the Den, which only give you gills for a few minutes, so they will be far more useful if we suddenly find ourselves hurled overboard all the way out here.'

He unscrewed the lid on the jar and he and Smudge each unwrapped a sweet and popped them into their mouths. Smudge winced. This watergum had a much stronger flavour than those she'd tried before. It had the consistency of a toffee, but it was salty instead of sweet and there was a lingering aftertaste of seaweed. Still, as Bartholomew said, it gave them both a better chance underwater if things got rough.

Smudge looked about the cabin. There was now a ship's wheel mounted on the wall to the left of the steps and as she wandered over to it she saw that each spoke had a different destination engraved into it: **eastmost**, **southmost**, **westmost** and, finally, **northmost**.

'The poem on the map mentioned the **northmost star**,' she whispered. 'Perhaps each of these destinations is a different star ...'

She took hold of the spoke engraved **northmost** and turned it in a full circle. The boat lurched forward and Smudge's face brightened. Her guess, it seemed, had been right and once again they were on their way! Smudge grinned at Bartholomew, who gave a shaky thumbs up in response, then they set about exploring the rest of the cabin as **The Coddiwomple** sailed on through the night towards the Fallen Crown.

After marvelling at a cutlass that became invisible when touched and a jar filled with eyeballs that followed their every move, they settled down to sleep – Smudge tucked up in the cubbyhole bed and Bartholomew inside the top drawer of the chest of drawers snoring far too loudly than was considered polite for an animal of his size. But Smudge had accidentally travelled with a belonging from home, after all, and on realising she had her earplugs in her tunic pocket (she was well used to Bartholomew's snoring back at Littlefern) she had tucked them in, closed the curtains across the window and lain down to sleep. She slept soundly until one of her earplugs slipped out halfway through the night and she happened to brush aside the curtain in search of it.

There was a face pressed up to the glass: a woman's face with pale skin, barnacled lips, seaweed hair and a crown of bones.

A shiver crawled through Smudge, but she looked on, spellbound, because this was a sea witch – Smudge had read about them in Nefarious Flood's diaries. They were rumoured to be some of the rarest creatures in Crackledawn and legends said that they wore gowns stitched from drops of moonlight and stank of rotten fish, but little more was known about them and from the expression on this one's face, Smudge got the impression that they weren't altogether friendly in nature.

She swallowed. What did the sea witch want? Smudge made to alert Bartholomew, but then the sea witch opened her mouth. And even through the window Smudge could hear the ghostly call of its voice as well as the dozens of others that seemed to join it and echo round the boat: high-pitched whines, like wind rattling through the stonework of a very old building.

Smudge's limbs slackened and her head slumped back onto the pillow as she fell into a cursed sleep, while on the floor, Bartholomew's body became limp too as he succumbed to the witches' song.

Five intense giggles came moments later up on deck, then the creak of the trapdoor opening and footsteps stealing down the stairs as a sea witch entered the cabin. The witch curled her lip in disgust at the snoring monkey, but her eyes glinted at the sight of the girl in the bed and she stalked towards the cubbyhole, dripping water from her moonlit gown. She peeled back the covers, lifted Smudge out of bed and carried her up the stairs.

'Sisters,' she hissed as she climbed back

through the trapdoor. 'I have her, as Morg commanded. She will be our prisoner until the harpy comes.'

One by one, a dozen bony hands curled round the edge of the boat. Then faces appeared – more barnacled lips and sunken cheeks – as the swarm of sea witches reached up and pulled Smudge down into the sea.

But what the witches didn't realise, as they swam towards their shipwreck at the bottom of the ocean, was that their curse hadn't sunk inside Smudge quite as deeply as they had hoped. The girl still had one of her earplugs in and, though she couldn't move her limbs, her mind was very much alert – and terrified.

She was breathing underwater – the watergum had given her gills, as it had promised – but it had also promised her the ability to talk, which would give her means of negotiation with the witches.

Then Smudge remembered the wording on the label: **allow several hours for optimum effect.** She didn't have hours to wait! She needed to speak now – to try and reason with the sea witches somehow – but, when she opened her mouth, no sound came out. She opened her eyes instead, as much as she dared, and with rising panic she watched as she was hauled deeper and deeper into the sea.

Chapter 10

Smudge could taste the fear at the back of her throat. Surely the watergum would release all its magical properties soon? But, even if it did, what could she say that would help her cause against these creatures who were working for Morg? Smudge tried to think clearly. Perhaps she needed to wait a while for the curse on her limbs to wear off before hatching a plan? Because, if talking didn't help, she'd need to be ready and able to make a quick escape some other way.

She kept half an eye on the swarm of

sea witches around her as they pulled her down into the ocean. They were still calling to one another, their eerie cries trailing through the water, and Smudge wished that Bartholomew was by her side. They weren't quite friends yet – she supposed there was more to friendship than holding hands for a moment in a sinking ship – but they were comrades in this quest. Although Smudge knew that, if Bartholomew did wake from the witches' curse, he'd have no idea where she'd gone. And, even if he had seen, white-nosed monkeys were petrified of deep water, and she reckoned he'd only actually trust the watergum if she was right beside him.

A horrible feeling stretched inside Smudge. What if Bartholomew never woke up? What if he met his end alone and stranded on a boat at sea? Or, what if he woke, but didn't try to find her? He could just sail **The Coddiwomple** back to

Wildhorn and that would be that. After
all, he had wanted to return home all
along ...

Smudge blinked the thought away. The
idea of being left alone at the mercy of
Morg was just too much. She had to try
and escape the sea witches and hope
that Bartholomew would still be aboard
The Coddiwomple, waiting for her. Through
slitted eyes, she watched the gloomy shape
of a wreck draw near.

The ship was tilted into the seabed,
its deck swamped in seaweed, its mast
clamped with barnacles. There was only a
scrap of sail left and that was covered in a
veil of slime.

The witches glided into the vessel and
down the sweeping staircase. Perhaps
once it had been grand, with polished
banisters and carpeted steps, but now it
was a slope of rotten wood scattered with
silt. At its foot there was a long-abandoned

ballroom with chandeliers draped in kelp and marbled pillars lost in seagrass. There were more sea witches here, reclining on threadbare chaises longues and seated at card tables covered in gloomweb – steel-strong gossamer spun by the elusive, almost extinct gloomcrab.

The witches around Smudge spilled out into their lair to join the rest of their kind, all except the one with the crown of bones who had pulled Smudge from her bed. She was silent now, but her fingers were still wrapped round Smudge's wrist and through half-shut eyes Smudge watched as she made her way towards the far end of the room.

'Let's take you over to Recycling,' the sea witch muttered. 'Morg will be here for you soon.'

Smudge's stomach clenched at the harpy's name. She tried to piece things together. The witches were working for

Morg – that much was clear – but what were they recycling way out here?

Smudge risked opening her eyes a little further so that she could see more clearly. The end of the room which they were heading towards was even more overgrown than the rest of the place. Waist-high weeds swayed with the current, and dotted here and there among them Smudge noticed several wooden caskets. The caskets were empty, but something about their shape seemed familiar. And unfriendly ...

Then Smudge's skin chilled at the realisation of what was unfolding in the ballroom. She had thought that all the creatures in there were sea witches, but now she could see that in fact there were only about ten witches here. The rest – those lying on the chaises longues, propped up at the card tables and waltzing through the grass with the sea witches – were skeletons. And the wooden caskets were **coffins**.

This was an underwater graveyard!

Smudge's thoughts spun. Was the witch planning to keep her in a coffin, surrounded by the dead, until Morg came to finish her off? With everything in her, Smudge tried to move as the witch dragged her into the midst of the open caskets – but it was useless. The curse held fast. So Smudge was left with no choice but to watch as the witch ran a finger over the words carved into the upturned floorboards that acted as tombstones before each coffin.

'No point depositing you in a **Definitely Dead** casket,' she said. 'They're reserved for our special guests – those who arrive without a pulse. So **Annoyingly Alive** it'll have to be. Until Morg gets here anyway.'

Smudge's pulse skittered. The sea witches were recycling **bodies**. She scrunched her eyes shut as the witch bundled her inside the casket, laid the lid back on top, then hummed to herself as she drifted away. When Smudge was sure that the witch was gone, her eyes sprang open.

The casket lid was wooden, but chunks of it had rotted away and Smudge peered through the gaps, trying to figure out how to escape. She needed a plan – and fast – because who knew when Morg would arrive ...

'If you were smart enough to swallow a watergum **beyond** the Northswirl, then your voice will come back first, followed, rather unhelpfully, by the feeling in your leftest toe.'

Smudge's eyes swivelled to the edge of the casket to her right, where the man's voice – crystal clear, despite the water around them – had unmistakably come from.

'Unless the watergum was faulty,' the

man continued, 'in which case I believe the sea witches' curse will sink into your bones at the next full moon. Then it'll be time for a casket upgrade – a perk for non-pulsers apparently – as you charge on through to **Definitely Dead**.'

Smudge felt a mix of panic and horror swirl inside her as she read the words engraved at the head of the coffin next to her: **Annoyingly Alive**. Who was this man? A sailor from a land beyond the Northswirl? How long had he been festering away at the bottom of the sea? And had she eaten a faulty watergum meaning the sea witches' curse would eventually kill her even if she managed to escape Morg?

Smudge focused on listening to the witches, in case she could glean anything else about the harpy. One of them was now playing a ghostly tune on a violin which echoed through the ballroom, but as Smudge listened she felt a tingle in her throat, like that of breathing in icy air on a winter's day. Then her tongue started to feel looser and her jaw slackened and finally, to her surprise, she found that she could feel the little toe on her left foot. Smudge gasped with relief. The curse hadn't sunk into her bones and, as she let out the tiniest of croaks, she knew that the watergum had, finally, worked its full magic!

Smudge glanced at the casket next to her because here was someone who obviously knew what he was talking about and who she could use as a sounding board for an escape plan.

'After the feeling comes back to your leftest toe,' Smudge whispered, 'what's next?'

There was a dry laugh. 'Next? Oh, there's nothing after that. **Annoyingly Alive** is – as the name suggests – frightfully annoying. You might have a pulse – which

means that at least the sea witches
won't go throwing you around in a waltz
or feeding you sea slugs on the chaises
longues – but you can't move. Other
than your leftest toe – and that novelty
soon wears off. Twenty years I've been
Annoyingly Alive among a graveyard of
Definitely Deads, if my memory serves me
correctly – it's been a while since I ended
up here.'

'Who are you?' Smudge asked.

There was a pause from the other
casket. 'It doesn't matter any more – I'm
a nobody now ...' The man took a deep
breath. 'Down here, it's just about sitting it
out, girl. Sitting it out until the bitter end.
Unless you're a magical beast – in which
case I believe a strong sunrise can break
the curse.'

For a second, Smudge felt relieved as
she thought of Bartholomew, bewitched on
the boat, but in with a chance of waking

up come sunrise. But would he hang around or would he sail back to Wildhorn, as she feared?

Smudge shut the thought out. 'I can't just sit it out,' she hissed. 'The Rising was meant to happen two nights ago but it went horribly wrong. And now the Unmapped Kingdoms don't have a new phoenix and there's a harpy called Morg on the prowl who's set on draining all the kingdoms of magic.'

'Is Crackledawn still standing without a renewal of the phoenix's magic?' The man sounded surprised and scared as if, just possibly, he knew a little more about Crackledawn than he was letting on.

Smudge thought about his question. 'It is – just – but it won't be for much longer ... There's only me and a grumpy monkey called Bartholomew who aren't under a Nightdagger curse sent by the harpy. So, if I give up, Crackledawn will fall to dark magic and so will the rest of the kingdoms, and the Faraway will perish! I set out from Wildhorn to stop the creature so that's what I'm going to do.'

There was a pause from the other casket. 'You sound a little young to be tackling harpies.'

'Yes,' Smudge replied tartly, 'I know. I'm under-age and very probably under-intelligent, too. But I'm trying my best. And Bartholomew says I'm capable of extraordinary, impossible things.' She paused. 'I haven't got much of a plan now, but there's a niggle inside me and it won't give up.'

'A niggle, eh?' The man sighed. 'I used to be full of niggles, but look where they got me. The bottom of the sea.' He took a deep breath. 'I'm afraid I don't think anything can get us out of this scrape – once a sea witch's curse weasels into your ears, it's notoriously hard to shake ...'

Smudge cleared her throat. 'Well, it's a good job Bartholomew snores then.'

'Who on earth **is** this monkey? And what have his nasal passages got to do with anything?'

'I'm wearing an earplug,' Smudge whispered. 'You have to if you want to get a full eight hours' kip in the same hammock as a white-nosed monkey snoring his head off. But I think the earplug blocked out some of the sea witches' curse because I can feel more than my leftest toe now.' Smudge grinned. 'I can feel my fingers –' she clenched her fists – 'and my arms. And I'm going to get us both out of this mess.'

There was a stunned silence from the casket beside her, then a roguish chuckle. 'Well now, that rather puts the ball back in our court.'

Smudge jumped as a high-pitched bell rang through the ballroom.

'They'll be putting the skeletons back to rest now,' the man said. 'That's how it usually goes – because apparently even the **Definitely Dead** need some downtime.'

But Smudge's mind wasn't on the man's words. Her head was filled with sideways thoughts – with the **what ifs** and the **just maybes** of their situation – and an idea was surfacing.

'Sounds are important in Crackledawn,' she said quietly. 'The seas are full of sun-chatter – low **and** high-pitched noises. But, down here, every single sound – the witches' cries, the violin and even the bell – seems to be high-pitched ...'

She fell silent as she heard the witches sashay round the caskets, settling the skeletons down to rest. When she was sure they had swum away, Smudge spoke again.

'What if there's a reason for that? Maybe a low sound would break their

magic and lift the curse on both of us?'
She paused. 'I don't have time to wait
until every part of my body starts moving
again – I need to act **now** in case Morg is
close. So what do you think? Could a low
sound help?'

The man said nothing for a while. 'Your
idea isn't all bad – in fact, it makes a lot of
sense. In a book I once read, **Secrets of a
Sea Witch** by Montgomery Dampweed, it
talked of a sailor who encountered a sea
witch and used a net full of low-pitched
sun-chatter – chimney moans and bottom
A notes from a piano, I believe – to fight
it off. But those kind of sounds usually
only grow around reefs and we, as you
well know, are trapped in a wreck on the
ocean floor.'

'But there are sounds down here, all
the same,' Smudge said. 'Maybe not the
ones you catch in raiding nets. But –' she
watched the seagrass sway above the

coffin as her mind ticked over – 'there are magical beasts here. Creatures who make sounds. And there's one creature responsible for the lowest sound of all – lower than the bottom note on a piano, lower even than thunder.'

'You want to summon a **whale**?'

'Not just any old whale but the whale with the lowest song in Crackledawn.' Smudge took a deep breath. 'I want to summon a silver whale.'

Chapter 11

The man in the casket laughed. 'Never in all my time at sea have I heard of a person summoning a silver whale. They're as wild as sea dragons – they don't just appear on demand. And besides, even if you **were** to whistle for one – as Henrietta Humpleback, who claimed to be a whale whisperer (despite having no luck whatsoever calling silver whales), instructed – you wouldn't manage it.' He sniffed. 'Because you'd need an item of silver under your tongue while whistling. And if Henrietta Humpleback had read

Gertrude Scatterworth's **Fantastical Forgotten Facts** she might have had more luck.'

'Right then,' Smudge replied, but her words came out mumbled because, while the man had been jabbering on about Henrietta Humpleback and Gertrude Scatterworth, Smudge had been removing her nose ring and placing it under her tongue in a desperate attempt to summon a whale.

'Why do you sound as if you've got a crab wedged in your throat?' the man asked.

Smudge ignored him and began to whistle. And, though the sound was soft and almost lost in the prattle of the sea witches in the ballroom, it rang out all the same.

'You've evidently managed to conjure up some silver,' the man said, 'which is impressive, but I wouldn't get your hopes up for the next bit. I really think silver whales have better things to be doing with their time than heeding the call of the **Annoyingly Alive**.'

Smudge whistled again for the silver whale and, as she did so, she poured all the hope she had inside her into her breath. Because if there was one thing she was learning out here on the open seas it was that self-belief was almost as powerful as magic.

Suddenly a hush fell over the ballroom as the witches' chatter faded away. Smudge fell silent, too. But she needn't have worried. The sea witches' anxious silence was not caused by her whistling, which they hadn't even heard above their chattering, but by the silver glitter that had started floating down the staircase and drifting in through the glass-less windows.

Smudge held her breath as flecks of silver dropped through the holes in her casket and she found herself remembering Bartholomew's words. **Seawater can change colour depending on the types of creatures that swim in it. Silver for the silver whales ...** Smudge hoped hard. Could it be that a silver whale had heard her call?

Then a new sound rumbled across the floorboards. A long, slow boom that juddered through the ship as if it was made of paper. Smudge's heart leaped. Only a silver whale could make a sound that low! Again came the whale's echoing song and the noise seemed so close Smudge felt it thrum in her bones. And, as the call swelled round the boat, Smudge felt the power return to her body at last.

She burst out of the casket just as the man in the coffin beside her did the same. Only now he was brilliantly alive! He had shining green eyes and was running his hands over his matted beard and torn tunic, as if he could hardly believe that they belonged to him. Smudge blinked. It couldn't be ...

And yet it was. Next to her stood **Nefarious Flood**. Her all-time hero. And, up until Smudge and Bartholomew's voyage, the only person to have sailed beyond the Northswirl! Smudge blinked once, twice and then a third time. He was still alive, after all this time! He hadn't drowned as everyone thought ... He had been a prisoner of the sea witches all along.

Then, out of the corner of her eye, Smudge glimpsed something else. An enormous creature with skin so silver it would have made starlight look dull. The silver whale glided past the window then disappeared, and only its song was left, reverberating through the wreck.

With the whale gone, the sea witches turned their attention to Smudge and Nefarious and the group began to advance towards the two escaped prisoners. Smudge froze. She realised that she had absolutely no idea what to do now that she was free. The witches rushed towards her ...

Crash!

The wreck juddered with such force Smudge and Nefarious were knocked to the ground and the sea witches smashed against the pillars.

'The silver whale,' Nefarious gasped. 'I don't think it's gone yet ...'

There was another ear-splitting crash and Nefarious grabbed Smudge by the arm as a chunk of ceiling collapsed beside them.

'Swim!' he yelled. 'Swim!'

Together they headed for the staircase, but the witches were on their tail, refusing to give up their prey so easily. The silver whale was making life difficult for them, though, and it was only when Smudge and Nefarious were up on deck that they saw how. The whale was thrashing its mighty tail against the wreck and, as Smudge and Nefarious dodged out of its way, the whale turned its tail on the witches that tried to follow them.

The witches sang to try and push the silver whale back, but the creature was fighting with a wilder magic than theirs and it flung its tail at any witch that came close and sang out its booming notes, draining the witches of their power. And as Smudge and Nefarious kicked away from the wreck, the sea witches' song weakened to nothing until one by one they sank back into the depths of the ocean.

Hardly daring to believe their luck, Smudge and Nefarious kept swimming upwards. Then Smudge's eyes grew very, very large because, instead of water against her belly, she felt the cool, smooth touch of whale skin. She gasped as the wonder of things danced inside her. Because here she was, beyond the

Northswirl, riding a silver whale with Nefarious Flood!

She turned to the Sunraider behind her, who was running a hand over the whale's dorsal ridge and blinking in astonishment.

'I have seen many things in my lifetime,' he murmured, 'but none so extraordinary as this.'

Smudge smiled and deep inside her, in the slightly overlooked and under-cherished corner of her heart, she felt something stir. It could have been pride or maybe it was simply joy. Whatever it was, it had happened because she had dared to believe not only in the impossible but in herself.

Smudge faced forward and watched, in silent awe, as the whale carried them through the sea. They passed an octopus that blew golden bubbles and a stingray that changed colour every time it flapped its fins, but nothing was as magnificent as the whale they rode on. It was like riding a giant, or a fallen star, and it was so soul-smashingly magical that Smudge had to bite down on her lip to stop herself squealing.

Eventually, though, shards of sunlight filtered down from the surface of the sea and from the angle they fell Smudge could tell that it was already midday. She thought of Bartholomew. Had the sunrise woken him up, as Nefarious had suggested? And was he waiting for her to return or – Smudge's throat tightened – had he turned tail and fled to Wildhorn?

Smudge hoped and hoped and hoped again as the whale broke through the surface of the sea, sending a torrent of water out through its blowhole, then Smudge's face broke into a wide smile. Because there was **The Coddiwomple** and, at its helm, an extremely anxious-looking monkey, chewing on a trilby.

'Bartholomew!' Smudge shouted.

'Oh, Smudge!' the monkey cried. 'You haven't gone and died, after all!'

The silver whale raised its magnificent head towards the bow of the boat and Smudge and Nefarious clambered off. Bartholomew flung his arms round Smudge, then remembered himself and let go.

'Please don't hug me in front of company, Smudge,' he tutted. And then his eyes widened as he, too, realised quite who the company was. 'Nefarious Flood! Well, I never ...'

Nefarious laughed as he ran a hand over the side of the dhow. 'Didn't think I'd be seeing this old girl again.'

Smudge leaned over the boat until her face was level with the silver whale's. Its eye was small and almost lost in the wrinkles and the barnacles that surrounded it, but it shone as bright as the sunrise.

'Thank you,' Smudge whispered.

The silver whale dipped its head and as it did so Smudge felt a tingling sensation on either side of her neck. She raised her hands and to her surprise, she felt little ridges under her skin there. Her gills! They hadn't disappeared completely, as they did with ordinary watergums. Now they were with her forever, just under the surface, and she would remember, every time she dived underwater and used them, the silver whale that had answered her call. The whale sank below the surface until all that remained on the water was a patch of silver bubbles.

'So,' Bartholomew mused as he placed his hands on his hips and stared at Smudge. 'You disappeared in the middle of the night – from the stench in the cabin and the fact I couldn't move a muscle I assumed the sea witches had taken you. When the sun rose, I was freed from their curse, by which time **The Coddiwomple** had drifted and I had no idea where you might be. But here you are, on the back of a silver whale with a Sunraider who's been dead for almost twenty years!'

Smudge nodded. 'It's been a busy few hours.'

Bartholomew raised an eyebrow, then he turned to Nefarious who was stroking the dragonhide sail. 'Thank you for rescuing Smudge. I do try to keep her under control, but she is, I fear, utterly unmanageable.'

Nefarious laughed. 'Rescuing her? I did no such thing. It was Smudge here who rescued **me**.'

Bartholomew turned to Smudge. 'How on earth did you manage that?'

'Whistling mostly,' Smudge replied.

Nefarious sat down on a broken bench. 'Turns out Smudge here probably isn't going to make a very good Sunraider.'

Smudge's face fell. Nefarious had only

just met her and already he had decided she was a hopeless case. She had thought he'd been impressed with her plan, but obviously he'd noticed something especially useless about her down in the wreck ... Something unfixable that meant she wasn't cut out for anything of note.

She glanced over at him, but Nefarious didn't seem to look displeased or disappointed, as the Lofty Husks often did. In fact, he was looking hopeful and just a tiny bit mischievous.

'I know I never was,' he said quietly, and smiled.

Bartholomew looked up from bailing out the water the silver whale had blown into the boat. 'But you went down as one of Crackledawn's greatest Sunraiders!'

Smudge nodded. 'There are books on you and everything – and there's a portrait back in the Den!'

'Is there now? I hope they captured my

devilish good looks and roguish charm.'
Nefarious made room for Smudge on the
bench beside him. 'People – well, grown-
ups in particular – are very fond of labels.
You're either this or you're that. A Sunsmith
or a Sunraider. But, the truth is, I was never
a terribly good Sunraider. I got some truly
dreadful exam results, despite trying my
hardest, and I almost never returned from
raiding trips on time and with the right mix
of sun-chatter.'

Smudge's heart skipped a beat.
Nefarious Flood, the most famous Sunraider
in Crackledawn, sounded just like her! She
grinned at the knowledge that someone
brilliant, legendary even, had started out
in just the same faltering way as she was.

'It sounds like you think differently from
most people, Smudge, but that is certainly
not a bad thing. The world needs people
to look at things from different angles;
that's what keeps it moving forward.' He

smiled at Smudge. 'You and I are made of the same stuff.'

Smudge leaned forward eagerly. 'What's that?'

'Curiosity, courage and self-belief. And do you know what that makes us?'

'Criminals?' Bartholomew asked.

Nefarious laughed. 'No, my dear Bartholomew, it makes us **explorers**. You and I, Smudge – we're destined for voyages to far-flung places and adventures at the edges of our world.'

Bartholomew groaned. He wasn't sure he approved of the direction the conversation was taking: it was one thing telling Smudge to believe in herself, but quite another encouraging her to go on explorations to the ends of the earth.

'We might not know quite where we're heading most of the time,' Nefarious went on, 'which is actually why I named my ship **The Coddiwomple**—'

'Isn't a coddiwomple a type of limpet?' Bartholomew interrupted sourly.

'Coddiwomple is one of the finest words in the dictionary,' Nefarious replied. 'It means to travel purposefully in a vague direction.' His eyes roamed the sea around them. 'So, Smudge, do you have a destination in mind for this mission?'

'Everdark,' Smudge said quietly, 'via the Fallen Crown, according to **The Coddiwomple**, though I'm not really sure what that is. We know Morg has returned to Everdark to brew a curse for me and Bartholomew, but unless we get there before she makes the curse we risk the harpy taking control of Crackledawn, then flying on to the other Unmapped Kingdoms to steal their magic, too.' Smudge paused. 'Wings are power for a harpy, so Morg said back at Lonecrag, so if we can somehow steal Morg's wings then maybe we're in with a chance of stripping her of her power.'

Nefarious nodded. 'Then we must sail on with curiosity up our sleeves, courage in our hearts and –' he shot a sideways glance at Smudge – 'in the firm and rather exciting knowledge that we have on board our boat one of the most ingenious minds in Crackledawn.'

Smudge had no idea what **ingenious** meant, but from the grin on Nefarious' face, and the despair plastered all over Bartholomew's, she decided it must be a compliment. All her life she had been ashamed of thinking differently from everybody else, but she was beginning to see that it wasn't such a disaster, after all. By thinking differently, she had sailed beyond the Northswirl, escaped a swarm of sea witches, rescued Nefarious Flood – and now she was back on course to stop Morg.

Chapter 12

Down in the cabin, over a cup of jungleleaf tea, Nefarious talked Smudge and Bartholomew through the tails mounted on the walls.

'A hydra I bumped into while crossing the Northswirl.' He held up his right hand that, Smudge noticed, only had four fingers. 'The hydra took the fifth,' he said darkly.

Smudge listened, wide-eyed. Nefarious Flood was every bit as marvellous as she had imagined, and hearing about his adventures first-hand was so thrilling her toes had started to tingle. She felt more confident about what lay ahead now, too, because here was a man who had brought down hydras and krakens – he'd be a match for the harpy ...

Nefarious pointed to a purple tentacle coiled up on the plaque above his desk. 'This kraken here tried to drown me shortly after the Northswirl and I showed him who was boss.' He winked. 'Until the wretched thing came back for me the next day – turns out you've got to take more than a tentacle from these creatures if you want them off your back – capsized my boat and sent me down to the sea witches' wreck. But losing thumbs and boats is all part of being an explorer. If we make it back from Everdark with our toes intact, I shall be most surprised.'

Bartholomew choked into his teacup. 'How about a jollier subject for the journey, hmmmm?'

But there's a limit to how light you can keep the conversation when you're sailing towards trouble. And, though nobody said anything as dusk fell and the sea grew darker, Smudge, Nefarious and Bartholomew could sense each other's unease.

Smudge watched silently as a shiver of ghostsharks glided past the cubbyhole window – wisp-like creatures with hollow eyes and gaping mouths – followed by a jellyfish with feathered tentacles. Time drifted on, then Nefarious pointed as a flash of turquoise scales shot past the glass.

'It was only a glimpse,' he breathed, 'but it could just have been a sea dragon. This far north, the ocean is full of strange beasts.'

Smudge settled herself on the end of the bed – she didn't want to miss a thing – but no sea dragons appeared again and eventually she realised that the boat was slowing.

'We must be near,' she said quietly.

Bartholomew sat up straight in the obligasaurus. 'And we're none the wiser about what the Fallen Crown actually is ...'

Nefarious grabbed the merscale boomerang from the trunk. 'My enchanted object from the Lofty Husks when I was just a child,' he said when he saw Smudge frowning. 'I think we're going to need all the help we can muster.'

Before Smudge could ask what the boomerang could do, Nefarious flung open his wardrobe and pulled out a quiver of purple-fletched arrows and a bow. He slung the quiver over Smudge's shoulder. 'These arrows have taken down many a kraken in their time and, I think, are your best bet against Morg.'

'But ... but, I don't know how to use a bow and arrow,' Smudge stammered.

'Set the arrow against the string of the bow,' Nefarious explained. 'The tip of the arrow (which, by the way, is coated in frog poison) should be pointed at your adversary then simply pull back on the string and fire.'

Smudge grinned. Never in her wildest dreams had she imagined that Nefarious Flood would lend her one of his prized weapons!

'Let's take a look up on deck,' Nefarious added, hurrying up the steps as Smudge – almost as an afterthought – took a small jar she'd seen wedged inside the top drawer of Nefarious' desk and shoved it in her pocket. Then she and Bartholomew climbed up the stairs after Nefarious.

Smudge blinked at the beauty of the scene before her. The moon was up and the surface of the ocean was aglow with tiny blue lights belonging to the millions of plankton that swayed with the current and shone like scattered stars. Cutting a sharp silhouette against the sea of lights was a row of jagged rocks, twenty or so metres in length – in the unmistakable shape of a crown – and carved into the central rock there was a cave, lit green by glow-worm light, which shone out against the night like a jewel.

'Do you think this is it?' Smudge whispered. 'The Fallen Crown – the way through to Everdark?'

There was a clanking noise from the hull of **The Coddiwomple.**

'Is this the first time she's made that noise on this voyage or the second?' Nefarious asked.

'Second,' Smudge said, recalling the same strange sound after the dragonhide sail had changed before the Northswirl and the lantern had glowed blue at the bow.

'Oh dear.'

Bartholomew bit his tail. 'What does it mean? More whirlpools? Another fanged wave?'

'It means **The Coddiwomple** has already released its supply of merscales – most probably because you were being tailed by some deeply unfriendly sea monster – and now—'

The clanking sound faded, then there was a cracking noise, like that of wood splitting, as dozens of metal spikes burst through the wooden railings surrounding the boat.

Nefarious eyed his ship. 'We need to keep our wits about us. **The Coddiwomple** has cranked up its danger levels. We're now on High Alert.'

Bartholomew shivered. 'What's after High Alert?'

Nefarious looked him straight in the eye. 'Nothing. This is as dangerous as it gets.'

Smudge's heart fluttered with fear.

'We need to think this through,' Bartholomew said. 'We are poised before a cave that looks very much like it might be a gateway to Everdark, the most magical of places in all the Unmapped Kingdoms. So we should come up with a plan for what happens when we step through that cave and possibly find ourselves face to face with Morg.'

But **The Coddiwomple** didn't seem to care for forward planning and it lurched ahead, almost as if it was in a hurry, and, no matter how much Bartholomew, Smudge and Nefarious pulled on the sail ropes to try and slow it down, the boat charged on through the sea. And so focused were they all on watching the rocks ahead and working out whether they could get close enough to moor the boat and step ashore that none of them looked down to where the real danger lay.

Because where there are gateways to impossibly enchanted places there are usually gatekeepers, too. And this one had risen from the depths of the ocean at moonrise – no longer stunned by the merscales **The Coddiwomple** had released before the Northswirl.

The ogre eel sank beneath the boat, waiting for the right moment to pounce, and all the while **The Coddiwomple** threw everything it had at getting close to the glowing cave. But, no matter how many times it advanced, the waves grew, the current churned and they were spat right back to where they started.

'Let's try going round the side!' Nefarious shouted. 'Then we'll cut back in!'

And it was then that the ogre eel struck.

It burst out of the water, barring the way to the Fallen Crown, and everyone screamed at once as it sprayed foam and slime over the boat. Bartholomew gripped Smudge's waist as Nefarious yanked on the sail rope and manoeuvred **The Coddiwomple** backwards. The eel was vast, with flickering gills, a forked tongue and purple skin. And had it not been for the spikes that now lined the boat it would have thumped down and drowned them all that instant. For now, though, it lunged towards the mast, snapping it clean off and hurling the sail into the sea.

But, to the eel's irritation, the boat spun recklessly on towards the Fallen Crown, and Smudge, Bartholomew and Nefarious clung to the sides as it shunted into the rocks. There was a thud against the hull, then the sound of water pouring in.

'Jump now!' Nefarious yelled as the eel rose up again and shook its terrible gills. 'Before it's too late!'

Smudge clambered over the bow with Bartholomew, then they leaped on to the rocks and hoisted themselves away from the waves. But, just as Nefarious was readying to jump after them, an enormous wave smashed against the boat and dragged it backwards. Nefarious stumbled against a bench and the eel gathered itself up to its full height and hissed.

'Watch out!' Smudge screamed.

But, if there was one thing Nefarious was good at, it was fighting enraged sea monsters. He drew his arm back and hurled his merscale boomerang straight at the ogre eel. In a shimmer of scales, the weapon flew through the air and, though the monster swerved, the boomerang circled back to Nefarious and he hurled it again. This time the weapon caught the eel square in the face and, as the scales struck, the creature seized up, stunned. But it was too late. With no mast or sail, Nefarious couldn't move his boat and Smudge and Bartholomew watched, aghast, as the stupefied ogre eel thumped down on to **The Coddiwomple**, dragging it and Nefarious down into the sea.

'No!' Smudge yelled from the rocks. 'Nefarious!'

She scanned the water, but only a few pieces of broken wood lay strewn across the surface. And then ...

'There!' Smudge cried. 'Look!'

Nefarious burst through the water, coughing and spluttering, but he was alive. Very much alive. And there was something else, too: another boat in the distance sailing towards them. A large ship with a very round elf at the bow.

'**Dragonclaw?**' Smudge whispered. 'And – and is that Crumpet? But it can't be ... She was under Morg's curse – I watched it happen!'

Bartholomew blinked. 'And yet it **is** Crumpet.'

'Keep going, Smudge!' Crumpet roared as **Dragonclaw** drew closer. 'The only reason this kingdom is still standing is because of **you**! And the only reason I broke free from the Nightdagger curse is because the rock goblins piled aboard

Dragonclaw and whispered your name into my ear so many times that the hope bound up inside them – their belief in you – was enough to break the dark magic over me.'

Smudge took in the shadows of the other elves, lit up by the ship's lantern, still huddled round the warning bell.

'Their hope in you was enough to stir me, but the goblins couldn't wake the rest of the elves!' Crumpet shouted. 'When I asked **Dragonclaw**'s mind map how to get to Everdark to stop the dark magic that rose from there it told me only one Unmapper could go: the girl who sailed beyond the Northswirl and lived. Smudge, I think you're destined to do something extraordinary tonight! I followed you here to help give you the courage to keep going but I see now that you don't need me to do that – at whatever cost you will always go on!' She peered over the edge of the bow and gasped. 'Is ... is that Nefarious Flood?'

The swell shunted Nefarious further and further away from the Fallen Crown and towards **Dragonclaw.**

'Crumpet's right!' Nefarious panted. 'Keep going, Smudge. And you, too, Bartholomew! **Dragonclaw** will take me from here – and Crumpet and I can scour the books in the Warren to see if there's a way to wake the other Lofty Husks and preserve what's left of the phoenix's magic until a new one rises – but that light in the cave is dimming! I don't think you have long before it closes!'

Smudge glanced at the cave behind her. If the gateway was closing, did that mean she'd be stuck in Everdark forever? Her heart shook at the thought. Or were there more gateways and journeys ahead? Was that what it meant to be an explorer, as Nefarious had said – that she was destined for voyages to far-flung places and adventures at the edges of the world?

Smudge steeled herself as she looked at Nefarious. She **had** to be brave enough to go on without him, whatever lay ahead, because the fate of the Unmapped Kingdoms and the Faraway lay in her hands.

'This is **your** voyage now!' Nefarious shouted as another wave rammed him further from the rocks. 'Seize it with both hands!'

'I'll try!' Smudge cried. 'And thank you, Nefarious! I won't ever forget you! Or you, Crumpet!'

'I'll try my best to forget you, Nefarious,' Bartholomew wheezed as he scrambled over the rocks after Smudge, 'but I fear our harrowing encounter will remain seared on my brain forever.'

He gave Nefarious and Crumpet a shaky wave, then he followed Smudge into the cave as the light from the glow-worms closed in around them.

Chapter 13

Smudge wasn't sure when the cave
stopped being a cave and became a
forest, but, as she and Bartholomew walked
further inside it, it became clear that the
way back no longer existed. Gone were
the dripping walls of rock, gone was the
sound of roaring waves and gone was the
sight of **Dragonclaw** rushing to Nefarious'
rescue. Only shadows and trees remained,
and the near-silent heartbeat of a place
rarely visited.

Smudge tried to hold her fear at
bay. But Morg was somewhere in here,

brewing a curse to kill her. Smudge swallowed. She had seen trees back on Littlefern and Wildhorn – great jungled vines and arching palm trees – but they were nothing compared to the forest she stood in now. There was night beyond the trees somewhere – every now and again, Smudge caught a glimpse of the stars – but the forest was so deep and tangled that more often than not the way ahead and above and behind was completely masked by roots and creepers.

There were no birds, butterflies or buds, like perhaps there had been in the reign of the last phoenix. In fact, there was nothing living at all. This was a rotten forest. Fungus clung to the trunks and insects wove holes through decaying bark. Smudge drew the bow out of her quiver and, trying to remember exactly what Nefarious had told her, slotted an arrow in place. But thankfully, as she and

Bartholomew walked on, nothing stirred between the trees.

'Look at this one,' Bartholomew whispered shakily. 'I've never seen anything like it before.'

The tree to his left was bent right over, like an old man, and hanging from the branches were rusty keys.

'And that one ahead,' Smudge pointed.

It was hollow in the centre and many of the branches were now stumps, but from the few that remained there hung a collection of broken mirrors.

'I can feel the magic of this place,' Smudge breathed, 'but there's something sad about it – as if it's been left to go to waste. And if we don't stop Morg she'll do the same thing to Crackledawn ...'

There were more trees beyond these – ones that grew candles and coins and jewels – but every single one was dying. Smudge and Bartholomew crept further in and the hush deepened as they came upon a clearing. The trees surrounding it were dark and twisted, and one had a trunk so wide it contained a handful of doors carved into its bark, but it was the tree at the far end of the clearing, the one whose trunk was surrounded by dead birds and clumps of fungi, that made Smudge stiffen. Because where the branches split on this particular tree there was a nest.

The hairs on the back of Smudge's neck bristled. Everyone knew that phoenix nests were made from twigs and sun-beams, but this one was an enormous tangle of cobwebs and bones. And rising up from deep inside it was a strange green smoke.

Bartholomew clutched Smudge's arm as he took in the tips of the black feathers poking over the edge of the nest.

Smudge gulped. This was Morg's nest and it looked like she was home.

Bartholomew took a nervous step

backwards, but Smudge forced herself to stay where she was. Crumpet and Nefarious were relying on her and she needed to come up with a plan. She slid a glance to the tree with the doors. Some were rectangular, some domed and some small and circular, but each one bore an inscription on the front:

To Forgotten Dreams

To Faraway Stars

To Peace and Quiet

To Final Endings

And it was **this** door, with the dusty knocker and the chains draped over it, that Smudge was thinking about as she gripped her bow. Because, if she could pin Morg's feathers down in the nest – a considerable task considering she'd never fired a bow and arrow before – then maybe she'd be in with a chance of scrambling up the tree, stealing the harpy's wings and shutting them inside a door which very much implied that what went in would not be let out. Then, perhaps, Morg's power would crumble and a new phoenix would rise.

Her heart juddering at the scale of the task before her, Smudge tiptoed towards the harpy's lair and pulled back on her bow. She tried to ignore the sweat tingling in her palms and Bartholomew wincing behind her. Then she closed one eye, aimed and – with surprising accuracy – sent her arrow thwunking into the feathers.

A crow wing tumbled out of the nest and fell uselessly to the ground. Smudge frowned. Against the odds, she'd hit her target and yet ...

A sickening laugh rang out through the trees and two huge wings descended from another branch entirely, closing round Smudge like midnight. Smudge's scream died in her throat. The crow's wing had been a trap to lure her in while Morg watched, and waited, in the branches above.

'Get away from me!' Smudge cried as she thrashed her arms against the harpy's feathers.

But Morg's wings simply tightened round her, crunching her arrows into splinters of wood and making it impossible for Smudge to raise her bow to her chin. Smudge gasped as she felt the breath of the harpy on her neck and she realised that Nefarious' weapon was now utterly useless. She and Bartholomew had got this far – into the heart of Everdark and right up to Morg's nest – only to end up as the harpy's prisoners.

Smudge's thoughts spun wildly. What would happen if Morg dragged her up to her nest? How long would it take before the dark magic weaselled its way into Smudge's body? And how soon after that would the Unmapped Kingdoms crumble? Her heart shook at the thought of all the silver whales, sea dragons, rock goblins and Unmappers that would be no more. And all those continents in the Faraway that would perish.

'You dared to follow me into Everdark,' Morg hissed. 'You dared to think that **you**, a child, could defeat **me**?'

Smudge kicked out, but Morg held fast, locking her in a terrifying embrace as she dug her phoenix skull into Smudge's shoulder.

'I was planning to bring my curse to you,' Morg hissed, 'but, now that you are so conveniently in Everdark, I can simply drag you up to my nest where the darkest magic is brewing.' She laughed. 'Nestled inside those cobwebs and bones lies a spell made from a thousand nightmares and once it slips down your throat your pointless little life will be snuffed out like a candle. Gone. Forever.'

Morg wrapped a cold hand round Smudge's neck and, at the touch of those fingers, Smudge felt the hopes she'd carried with her all the way from Wildhorn drain from her chest. She cowered in Morg's grip, her eyes shining with terror, because there didn't seem room for curiosity, courage and self-belief now. All that felt useless in the face of such evil. Smudge gasped as the harpy readied herself to fly up to the nest. This was the end of her voyage and she was so alone and afraid that her spirit shook.

And that was when the white-nosed monkey started shouting.

'You're not alone, Smudge!' Bartholomew cried. 'I am your friend and I will not let you die!'

The monkey's voice sounded distant and faint, but the harpy's hold on Smudge's neck loosened for a moment.

'I told you the elves enchanted me with a voice **and** feelings!' Bartholomew bellowed. 'But I lied. They only gave me a voice. All the feelings – all the loyalty – grew because I have grown to understand that you are a brave and wonderful friend!'

The harpy growled, but still Bartholomew shouted and little by little his words kindled strength in Smudge's soul. When the monkey had held her hands in the Northswirl while **The Coddiwomple** sank, she had thought he was being kind because the elves had entrusted him with loyalty. But now he was telling her that they had done no such thing. Smudge had given up hope of making friends, but slowly, quietly, a friendship had been growing. And what a friend the white-nosed monkey was:

all he had wanted was to retire and live a safe, ordinary life, but instead he had followed her beyond the Northswirl and all the way to Everdark!

'I will never leave you, Smudge!' Bartholomew shouted. 'The same way Nefarious, Crumpet and all those goblins will never stop having faith in you! So don't give up now! Keep believing in the **what ifs** and the **just maybes** of this world. Because your spirit is bold – it revels in possibility – and **that** makes you infinitely powerful!'

And though the magic of the harpy was great, it seemed now that the magic of friendship – of unexpected loyalty and courage against the odds – was greater still.

Smudge threw all her strength at Morg at the same time as Bartholomew threw all of his. And, as Smudge bit and tore and punched, the creature jerked sideways and a gap opened up in her wings.

Chapter 14

Smudge seized her chance and charged through the gap in the harpy's wings only to see Bartholomew launching himself at Morg, teeth bared, claws splayed.

'Get away, pest!' Morg screeched.

But no matter how many times the harpy went to bat the monkey away he kept on coming back. Morg sprang into the air and for a second Smudge thought they had won, but then she realised the harpy was cackling to herself as she rose higher and higher in the sky.

'She's getting ready to dive!' Smudge

cried. 'So that she can drag me up to her nest!'

Smudge tried to think clearly and an idea began to take shape in her head. She reached inside her pocket, hurled the little jar she had taken from **The Coddiwomple** at Bartholomew and ran towards the nearest tree.

Bartholomew caught the jar and turned it over in his hands. 'You want me to catch Morg in a gloomweb? I thought recent events at Lonecrag showed us that nets and the like are a no go with harpies!'

'Stay there!' Smudge hissed. 'And ... and carry on being loyal!'

There was no time to explain the gloomweb – Bartholomew would have to figure it out – because Morg was rising up, up, up and Smudge knew that she couldn't afford to let her dive until she was ready.

Smudge scrambled up the branches of the tree, two at a time, flinching as she passed the green smoke fizzing from the harpy's nest. The forest rang with Morg's cries as she flew higher, and Smudge stumbled and slipped on the rotten wood, but she kept climbing. She hauled herself through the branches, past long-forgotten birds' nests and gnarled boughs, ignoring the stitch in her side and the thud of her heart. On and on she climbed until, finally, Smudge stood on the topmost branch of the tree.

She was above the canopy of the forest now and Everdark was spread out around her as far as she could see, a quilt of trees and rivers and towering mountains. The sky held the light of a million stars and spinning up into them was the silhouette of a harpy.

'And still you come!' Morg screeched.

Smudge steadied herself on the branch. 'Me and Bartholomew – we're not done with you yet!'

The harpy unfurled her wings, dipped

her skull and then dived straight for Smudge. But this was exactly what Smudge wanted. So, when Morg tore down towards her, Smudge twisted her body at the very last moment and threw herself on to the harpy's back.

The creature shook her body so violently that Smudge slipped and was left dangling from her talons. The harpy jerked and kicked, but Smudge clung on, desperately trying to claw her way up.

'If you fall, you'll die!' Morg shrieked.

'I'm not afraid to fall,' Smudge gasped as she dug her nails into the harpy's skin, wrenched her body upwards and swung round on to the creature's back. 'Because there's a white-nosed monkey on my side – and he's not going to let me down.'

Thankfully, Smudge was so high up in the trees she couldn't see Bartholomew who, right at that moment, was cursing because, having finally worked out how he could use the gloomweb, he now couldn't get the lid off the jar.

Morg swerved this way and that, but she couldn't shake the girl from her back. 'You're a nobody!' the harpy hissed. 'A powerless child who's seconds away from death!'

'Wrong,' Smudge spat. 'I'm an explorer who's seconds away from stealing your wings.'

Smudge yanked at the harpy's feathers and where the wings looped over the harpy's fingers they tore free before slipping backwards to reveal Morg's bony arms. Then both Smudge and the harpy were falling through the air – fast. Smudge wrenched hard on the wings and, though the phoenix skull remained clamped over the harpy's head, her wings broke away fully this time and Smudge pushed back from Morg.

They fell, side by side, through the air

and Smudge's heart thumped with fear.
Would her plan work? Or had she gambled
too much?

The harpy cried out – a hair-raising
scream – and, though she swiped for her
wings and lashed out with her talons,
this was not the same creature that had
spiralled into the sky earlier. She was
smaller without her wings, weaker, and,
while Smudge smashed down through the
branches as she fell, the harpy dropped
like a rag doll, with every branch punching
a little more of her strength away until she
came to a stop completely – a shrivelled
creature sprawled across a branch.

Smudge continued to plummet down
alone, clutching the wings that reeked of
mould and felt ice cold in her hands. She
careered past the cursed nest, but when
the ground rose up to meet her Smudge
smiled – because Bartholomew had worked
out what her plan was and, just in time,

had extracted the steel-strong gloomweb from the jar and strung it between the trunks of the trees at either end of the clearing.

The web broke the jolt of Smudge's fall, but she didn't hang around for a second because Morg, it seemed, was not dead after all but limping down through the branches after her. Smudge raced towards the tree with the doors carved into its trunk and, as if Everdark could sense there was a chance now to be rid of Morg, the chains hanging over the one marked **To Final Endings** fell away and the door itself swung open. Smudge hurled the wings inside, then slammed the door shut.

Morg screeched from the trees and the green smoke from her nest vanished, but the rusty chains hanging over the door were tightening back over it now. And the harpy and the girl, and even the monkey hyperventilating on the gloomweb, knew that this was a door that wasn't opening again.

Morg snarled, her eyes dark slits, and Smudge made to go after her. But the harpy scuttled away, like an overgrown spider, deeper and deeper into the forest. Smudge tried to follow, only to find the forest grew so knotted and wild that it was impossible to see where the harpy had gone and even harder to find the way ahead.

Smudge clambered back through the undergrowth and staggered into the clearing.

'You ... you did it,' Bartholomew stammered from the gloomweb. 'You saved Crackledawn!'

Smudge looked at him. '**We** did it, Bartholomew. And though the harpy might not be gone for good I think she'll be gone for a long time now she's lost the power of her wings. The Lofty Husks will awaken from her curse and, like Nefarious said, they'll see if there's a way to preserve what's left of the old phoenix's magic until a new one rises and Morg is killed for good.'

Bartholomew sniffed. 'Please would you come here immediately, Smudge.'

Smudge climbed on to the gloomweb and slumped down beside the monkey. 'Are you all right?'

Bartholomew brushed the tears away from his eyes. 'Quite all right, thank you, Smudge.' He paused. 'It's simply that I find myself in dire need of a hug.'

Smudge laughed as she wrapped her arms round her friend and for a while the two of them just sat there, on the gloomweb, looking up at the trees. A hush had fallen over Everdark, but the air felt different. Moonlight fell about the branches and moss and creepers glistened in its silver.

'Look, Bartholomew!' Smudge gasped. 'Look at the trees!'

Tiny candles appeared on the branches all around them, flickering quietly in the night.

'Everdark knows,' Bartholomew whispered. 'It knows that Morg has been beaten tonight. And that means all the Unmappers will know, too, because they will wake from her curse.' He paused. 'Then every cave in Wildhorn will echo with the news that on this day you and I did something extraordinary.'

Smudge beamed at his words. All those days finishing bottom of the class and being laughed at, all those nights spent crying into her pillow because she didn't fit in. And now this. A kingdom still standing because she had believed in herself.

'You said the Lofty Husks told you that one day I would sail you somewhere glorious,' Smudge said. 'I know you thought that meant retirement, but this –' she cast her arm around at the candles – 'well, it's a tiny bit glorious. Isn't it? To be the only two people in the whole of the Unmapped Kingdoms to have set foot in Everdark.'

Bartholomew smiled. 'It's more than a tiny bit glorious, Smudge.'

They watched the candles dance some more, then the monkey turned to his friend. 'With the gateway in the cave closed, I think we need to pick a door for ourselves now.'

Smudge nodded as they pushed up out of the web and walked towards the tree.

Bartholomew stroked the wood on the door marked **To Peace and Quiet**. 'This—'

'—will involve reading newspapers, having lie-ins and being bored. Sorry, Bartholomew, but I don't think it's a very good idea.'

They moved round to two more doors carved into the tree trunk. One was tall and rectangular and on it the word **Back** had been carved while the other was misshapen and battered-looking and it simply said **onwards**.

Smudge slid a glance at Bartholomew. 'We know what's on the other side of one of these doors.'

Bartholomew nodded.

'But all the **what ifs** and the **just maybes** aren't there.' She looked at the one marked **onwards**. 'They're in here.'

Bartholomew took a deep breath. 'I set out on this voyage thinking that I wanted to retire.' He paused. 'But now that Great-aunt Mildred's tea set and Uncle Jeremy's golf clubs are festering at the bottom of the ocean, I see that perhaps I have a little more living to do.' He held Smudge's hand. 'You see, dear Smudge, you have taught me that children, and monkeys, are curious and brave and – if they dare to believe it – stronger than sea witches, ogre eels and harpies.'

Smudge squeezed the monkey's hand,

then she raised her free hand to the door marked **onwards**. 'We have so much living to do, Bartholomew. So many places to discover, so many people to meet and so much more magic to unearth before the new phoenix rises.'

Bartholomew nodded and picked up his trilby, dusting it down and setting it on his head. Then together the girl and the white-nosed monkey pushed open the door and walked through.

About the Author

Abi Elphinstone grew up in Scotland where she spent most of her childhood building dens, hiding in tree houses and running wild across highland glens. After being coaxed out of her tree house, she studied English at Bristol University and then worked as a teacher in Africa, Berkshire and London. She is the author of **The Unmapped Chronicles**, **Sky Song** and

The Dreamsnatcher Trilogy. When she's not writing, Abi volunteers for Beanstalk charity, speaks in schools and travels the world – from the Arctic Circle to the mountains of Mongolia – looking for her next story.

You can find out more about Abi at www.abielphinstone.com and more about how YOU can help protect our environment at www.authors4oceans.org. You can also follow Abi on social media.

Facebook: www.facebook.com/abi.elphinstone
Twitter: @moontrug
Instagram: @moontrugger

On creating a dyslexic heroine in Everdark ...

The word 'dyslexic' doesn't exist in the Unmapped Kingdoms. The Lofty Husks probably took one look at it and decided it was far too difficult to spell, to bother remembering. But if it had existed, it would probably have been used to describe eleven-year-old Smudge. Late for everything, not much good at spelling, constantly daydreaming and always finishing bottom of the class, Smudge is an overlooked and largely forgettable girl – at the start of **Everdark**, anyway. But then she sets off on an adventure to save the Unmapped Kingdoms aboard a magical boat called **The Coddiwomple**, and she discovers that if she dares to believe in herself (and in magic) she might, in fact, be capable of extraordinary things.

The inspiration for Smudge came from my own childhood. At school I was branded 'unteachable'. Yes, I was a bit naughty (I see, in hindsight, that setting traps for your French teacher is unacceptable and stealing out of Maths lessons to run wild in the forest is unwise) but at the heart of this wayward behaviour was another issue. I was struggling in class to process information, structure my writing and concentrate, but I didn't know how to talk to my teachers about this and ask for help. I only discovered after school that I'm dyslexic.

I can't pin all of my childhood

naughtiness on my dyslexia, but I do think that it explains a few of the problems I had at school. I wish I'd known how to ask for help, I wish I'd learnt ways to make things a little easier and I wish I hadn't doubted my abilities so often. That said, I think coping with dyslexia at school – and finding my own methods to navigate it – has helped shape some of the strongest aspects of my character.

It took me seven years, three failed books and ninety-six rejection letters before I got my first book published. Although that journey was painful and embarrassing, it also taught me far more about joy and determination (not just in writing, but in life) than any of my good fortune ever has. Because inside every person who faces rejection there grows a quiet grit and a sense of joy at every little thing that **does** go right. Disappointing days stay firmly in perspective and I'd take that hard-won grit and joy over an easy book deal any day.

Since becoming an author, I've worked out various 'strategies' to make the writing process a little easier. Before I write a single word, I spend time gathering ideas. I read picture books, browse photography books, sketch maps and travel to new places to have adventures. I wander into antiques shops and inspect their treasures, such as grandfather clocks, glittering gemstones, leather-bound books and unusual keys. And I pinch character names from everyday things, like shower gel (cue the surname 'Pecksniff' of the heroine in **The Dreamsnatcher**) and street signs (cue 'Erkenwald' – the name of the magical kingdom in **Sky Song**, which came from a road in London).

When I've seen enough to inspire a story, I draw a map of the world I want to write about, because it is only when I start imagining my characters moving from place to place that a plot unfolds. Sometimes, I sketch my fictional world directly onto an Ordnance Survey map to make sure the geography works, and other times I draw onto a blank sheet of paper using memories of interesting places I've discovered. Often I get stuck when writing, those days when the words sit stubbornly out of reach, but I have never found myself stuck when doodling an imagined world.

I don't draw well, nothing is to scale and often the sprawling lines make no sense to anyone but me, but I am bold in my decisions. I'll have Wildhorn here (an island in Crackledawn complete with waterfalls that flow in figures of eight and feather-tailed monkeys that jump through the trees), I'll have Lonecrag there (home to ghastly ogre eels), and I'll have the

Northswirl beyond that (patrolled by sea witches). Maps tip me into my stories.

Once I've mapped a journey, I break my story down into bullet-pointed chapters (and sometimes sketches of key scenes), then I feel confident enough to take the plunge and start writing. I used to think that the people who were lucky enough to become authors were the people who scored the highest marks in class. But all you need to write a story, really, is an idea that nobody else has stumbled across yet and the determination to turn that idea into a book. And that is just as well for dyslexic people. Because we notice things other people miss and we know that if we dare to believe in ourselves we can be capable of extraordinary things.

The inspiration behind the Unmapped Kingdoms

The Unmapped Kingdoms started with a daydream, a **what if**, in my writing shed at the bottom of the garden. I thought back to all the incredible skies I'd seen on my book research adventures dog-sledding in the Arctic and living with the Kazakh Eagle Hunters in Mongolia: raspberry-pink sunrises, luminous sunsets, rain that summoned rainbows and made waterfalls roar, and snow that built jewellery out of spider webs. And I started wondering:

what if all the grown-ups have got it wrong about our skies? What if it isn't science and geography behind the weather, but magic? What if there are four secret kingdoms – Rumblestar, Crackledawn, Jungledrop and Silvercrag – filled with fantastical creatures who conjure weather for our world? Perhaps drizzle hags brew rain in giant cauldrons and snow trolls beaver away with moon syrup and cloud wisp to make snow? And so, the idea for the Unmapped Kingdoms came about ...

Each book in **The Unmapped Chronicles** is set in one of these four secret lands. In **Everdark**, you visit the sea kingdom of Crackledawn, complete with silver whales, rock goblins and underwater palaces. In **Rumblestar** you encounter a sky kingdom ruled by wizards with unending pockets from an enchanted castle built on the backs of sleeping cloud giants. In

Jungledrop, you dive into a glow-in-the-dark rainforest filled with gobblequick trees, golden panthers and parrots who repeat what you think, not what you say. And in **The Crackledawn Dragon**, you start off in a sea kingdom but before long you find yourself in Silvercrag with the sky stallions, frost giants and flyaway trees.

There's not an awful lot of time for sightseeing though, because Morg is on the loose and she'll stop at nothing until all of the Unmapped Kingdoms are under her power. And so it is up to various kids like Smudge in **Everdark**, Casper Tock and Utterly Thankless in **Rumblestar**, Fox and Fibber Petty-Squabble in **Jungledrop** and Zebedee Bolt in **The Crackledawn Dragon** to step in and sort things out ...

'**Adventures happen to people who need them. Whether they want them or not is entirely beside the point.**'

Turn the page for a sneak peek at the next
Unmapped Chronicles adventure...

Casper raised two shaking hands to his mouth. He was standing on a vast staircase that narrowed as it climbed upward. But what made his insides churn was the fact that the steps disappeared into a cloud and that either side of them there were clouds and that beyond the tree with the tangled roots that sprawled out over the steps, there were more clouds still.

Casper felt himself sway.

'Best not to get too close to The Edge,' the girl said, nodding towards the cloud the staircase seemed to be resting on. 'It's miles and miles down to the Boundless Seas and even though some of the most experienced Ballooners have launched off there in their hot air balloons, no one has **ever** tried to jump.'

Casper gave a shaky moan as the clouds around them shifted and he took in an unforgivably long drop down to the ocean. The water glinted in the afternoon sun and seagulls swung on the breeze and, had Casper not been hundreds of metres up in the sky, he could have almost imagined that the scene below was somewhere out in the North Sea. But then there was the staircase with the tree. And he felt perfectly certain that the trees in England, or indeed the trees in any other country on the world maps lining Mr Barge's classroom, did not sprout stationery, and they most definitely did not grow out of staircases in the sky.

The girl turned to face Casper and

he was surprised to see she was small, probably the same height as him. Somehow her attitude had made her seem bigger. 'Right, then,' she said. 'Would you like to be dragged up the steps by your ear or your hair? Both, I imagine, will be equally distressing.'

Casper spun back towards the door leading out of the tree. But it snapped shut as he reached for it and no matter how many times he tried to prise the wood open, the way into the tree, or the clock, or whatever it was, had closed.

Heart galloping, Casper turned around.

The girl gave a wicked smile and the stars on her cheeks glittered. 'I hope you're better with heights than Arlo.'

Casper clung onto the trunk of the tree. 'I'm not going anywhere until you tell me what on earth is going on. Where am I? Who are you? And on a scale of one to ten, how dangerous is Arlo?'

The little dragon wriggled out of the girl's pocket, fluttered upward, then blew hard through his nostrils. A puff of smoke trickled out.

Even so, Casper gulped.

Arlo flapped up to a branch on the tree and the girl pierced Casper with a haughty stare. 'He's a ten when he needs to be but he's got a bad chest so sometimes he finds breathing fire a bit of an ordeal.' She grabbed Casper by the scruff of his blazer and dragged him up a step. 'I'm Utterly Thankless and I'm a Bottler-in-training up at Rumblestar. I was **supposed** to be spending the afternoon in the castle but I got kicked out of class for flicking rain into my teacher's face. Silly old Blustersnap should have seen it coming when she asked me to do group work – you'd think she and the rest of the Lofty Husks would know by now that I only ever work alone. Still, it meant I sneaked out here for some peace and quiet and when I realised I was late for dinner I grabbed an envelope from the tree and was given a top-notch excuse for being out past curfew – capturing a criminal is important business, what with everything that's been going on!' Utterly paused on the step and looked at Casper. 'I was a **little** bit surprised at how easy you were to capture, though – just sitting there inside the tree looking hopeless – but perhaps you'll come into your own in the dungeons.'

Casper yanked himself free and clutched his hair. 'I'm not a criminal!'

Utterly rolled her eyes. 'Do you think it'll be quicker if I drag you or push you?'

'N ... neither,' Casper stammered. 'I'm staying right here because ... well ... I like rules too much to be a criminal, and I hate risks –' he grimaced at the staircase '– so climbing **that** is completely out of the question.'

Utterly sighed. 'You really are turning out to be a terrible disappointment, you know. I was expecting Morg's followers to be knife-wielding, karate-kicking, fire-breathing demons.'

Casper tried to block Utterly's ramblings out because they were bordering on madness now. **This must be a dream**, a voice in his head whimpered. **You've seen the world maps in Mr Barge's classroom and there's not a single mention of magical kingdoms. Surely you're just going to wake up any second and be back in Little Wallops, where**— Suddenly, Casper thought of his parents. He imagined them coming back to the flat and finding him gone. They'd be worried sick!

Utterly shook Casper by the shoulders and he snapped out of his thoughts. 'And how **can** you be scared to go up into Rumblestar when you've been nosing around and tampering with our marvels for

the past few weeks?' Her face darkened.
'Do you have **any** idea how hard it is to
catch marvels? They may look like ordinary
old marbles but they're flighty and fidgety –
they're the purest droplets of rain, snow
and sunlight after all!'

'I haven't been nosing around
anywhere!' Casper cried. 'I've been at
school trying my best to hand in homework
on time and avoid being hurled into a
bin. I know absolutely **nothing** about this
ridiculous-sounding Rumblestar.'

Utterly gasped at the insult, then
her words tumbled out, hot and angry.
'Ridiculous? **Ridiculous?** I'll have you know
that without Rumblestar, the Unmapped
Kingdoms would crumble! And then
who do you think would send sunlight to
Crackledawn, rain to Jungledrop and snow
to Silvercrag? The other kingdoms might
write the weather scrolls for the Faraway
but none of the continents there would exist

without Rumblestar **gathering** the marvels in the first place! Imagine a Faraway without rain to nourish the land, sunlight to make the plants and trees grow and snow to –' she paused '– cover Antarctica!'

Casper frowned at the mention of Antarctica. Why was this girl calling what sounded suspiciously like Earth the Faraway? He felt perfectly sure that Utterly was blurting out lies for one reason or another – magical kingdoms didn't exist and the world's weather did not rely on them – and yet he was realising that the angrier the girl got, the more information she gave away. So, if he could just keep baiting her, then maybe she'd come clean with what was **really** going on.

He took a deep breath and braced himself for the onslaught. 'Magical kingdoms aren't real and there are no such things as marvels of snow, sun or rain! Weather is based purely on scientific fact.'

'**Aren't real?**' Utterly spluttered. '**No such thing?**'

Up on his branch, Arlo covered his face with his claws.

'I suppose next you'll be telling me that none of the recent hurricanes in Europe happened? That there were no huge tornados in America? And that the whirlwinds in Africa and the typhoons in Asia and Australia were just rumours?' Utterly made a fist of Casper's shirt. 'When you swan into Rumblestar and start tampering with our marvels, it disrupts the entire weather system! How does it make you feel to know that because of **you** a hurricane flattened half of England earlier this week and –' she hung her head '– **killed** hundreds of people?'

Casper was far from ready to accept that he had stumbled into a magical kingdom and that events there were behind the recent weather-related disasters, but his face lit up at the mention of home.

'England!' he exclaimed, untangling himself from Utterly's grip. 'That's where I'm from! I go to a school there called Little Wallops—'

Utterly scowled. 'I'll wallop you if you're not careful.'

'Are you always this cross?'

'Cross is what happens when you burn toast or forget an umbrella.' Utterly paused. 'I'm not cross; I'm just unbelievably fierce.' She looked Casper up and down. 'You can't be from England. Everyone knows that those in the Faraway **stay** in the Faraway. They scurry around their continents doing non-magical things with non-magical people and non-magical creatures while those in the Unmapped Kingdoms **stay** in the Unmapped Kingdoms beavering away to make weather, because sharing the magic is what keeps the Faraway **and** the Unmapped Kingdoms turning!'

At this outburst, Casper glanced around hopefully for a grown-up but it was still just him and Utterly on the staircase, and Arlo in the tree. Clearly making Utterly even crosser was not the way to get her to speak logically. So, in a desperate bid to stamp some sense and order onto the situation, Casper lifted the crumpled timetable from his pocket and gazed at it longingly. What he would give to be doing his homework now, or even to be crouched inside the Lost Property basket or cornered in the library with Candida and Leopold. At least those situations made sense to him.

'What's that?' Utterly snapped.

Casper sighed. 'My timetable.'

'What's it for?'

'It tells me what to do when.'

'Doesn't your temper tell you that?'

Casper sniffed. 'I'd like to go home now, Utterly. To Little Wallops, where I'm from.'

Utterly hauled him up a few more steps. 'Criminals don't just go home. They get arrested, then tried, then fed to the dragons.'

'**What?**' Casper shrieked.

'Well, I'm not exactly **sure** that happens, but I'm pretty confident the Lofty Husks will want to put an end to you once they've tried you.'

Casper stood rooted to the step. 'In that case, I'm staying right here. On this step. Until everything goes back to normal.'

'I wouldn't,' Utterly smirked. 'Things can get pretty dangerous outside the castle walls after sunset.'

Casper looked at the cloud-strewn sky around them – he could have sworn he could hear something rumbling, like thunder, only that didn't make any sense because the clouds around them were wispy and white. Where on earth was he?

He brushed the strange noise aside and took a deep breath. Then, gripping the cuffs of his blazer so hard his knuckles turned white, he followed Utterly up the steps because the grandfather clock seemed to have disappeared completely and if all this **was** actually happening and he really **was** in some sort of strange place far away, then he was going to need help getting home, so he had to trust that maybe these Lofty Husks, whoever they were, would be more understanding than Utterly and listen to him when he explained that he wasn't a criminal but a boy who had got hopelessly lost ...

'Nothing, and I mean nothing,
is more powerful than a child in
possession of a plan.'

Get ready for another
breathtaking adventure in the
Unmapped Chronicles series

Dive into a magical quest beneath the ocean waves in the final **Unmapped Chronicles** adventure . . .

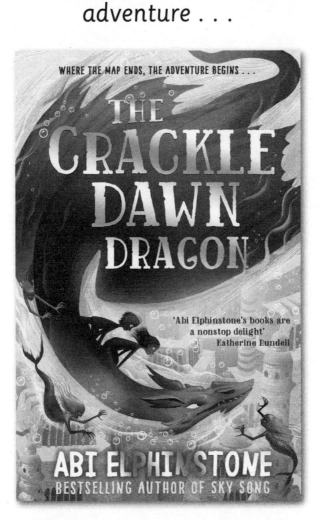

Publishing May 2021!